T0369338

ALL IT TAKES

ALL IT TAKES

STORIES BY

PATRICIA VOLK

ATHENEUM
NEW YORK

1990

SCRIBNER
Rockefeller Center
1230 Avenue of the Americas
New York, NY 10020

This book is a work of fiction. Names, characters,
places, and incidents either are products of the
author's imagination or are used fictitiously. Any
resemblance to actual events or locales or person,
living or dead, is entirely coincidental.

Some of these stories have appeared elsewhere, in slightly different
form:
"Rules and Laws" in *Apalachee Quarterly*; "The Yellow Banana"
in *The Atlantic* and *The Yellow Banana*; "Mystery Salad" (as
"Patricia Volk to Q") in *Quarterly*; "My Mother's Kiss" (as
"A Mother's Kiss") in *Present Tense*; "Blue Light" in *Quartro*;
"All it Takes" (as "Lake George With Crows"), "Reckless Dreamer"
(as "Unfinished Business"), and "Seams" in *The Yellow Banana*;
and "The High-Bouncing Lover" (as "The Hat Wall") in *Stories
About How Things Fall Apart And What's Left When They Do.*

SCRIBNER and design are trademarks of Macmillan Library Research USA, Inc. under
license by Simon & Schuster, the publisher of this work.

Designed by Diane Stevenson/Snap-Haus Graphics
Manufactured in the United States of America

Library of Congress Cataloging-In-Publication Data
Volk, Patricia.
        All it takes : stories / by patricia Volk.
              p.   cm.
        ISBN: 0-7432-3761-7
        I. Title.
    PS3572.0393A45   1990
813'.54—dc20   89-15132   CIP

10 9 8 7 6 5 4 3 2 1
Printed in the United States of America

For information regarding the special discounts for bulk purchases, please contact Simon
Schuster Special Sales at 1-800-456-6798 or business@simonandschuster.com

TO JO

For their hospitality I would like to thank the Corporation of Yaddo, the MacDowell Colony and the Mercantile Library of New York.

I am especially grateful to Andy, Peter and Polly and Audrey and Cecil Volk, Starr Scott Brin, Carmela Cangialosi, Erika Goldman, J. R. Humphreys, Judy Kern, Bambe Levine, Allen Woodman and the first person to recommend me books, Marjorie Saunders Levenson.

Nothing that we love overmuch
Is ponderable to our touch.

CONTENTS

ALL IT TAKES

MYSTERY SALAD

My sister Sukey calls to tell me You don't sound
so good.

I tell her I've been carrying around a prescription
for Prozac for two weeks.

"I once carried around a prescription for Clomid
for a year," she says.

"The stuff they put in pools?"

"That's good," Sukey says. Her laugh has no
build. Neither has mine. It's no surprise. Sukey is
more than my older sister. She is my trailblazer. I
never needed an abortion until Sukey had hers. She
pierced her ears at a time when the only place you
saw that was *National Geographic*. Now I think I
am waiting for her to get a divorce so I can contemplate one of my own. The more things Sukey does
I wind up doing, the more I sense the inevitability
of not doing anything she hasn't done. I hope she
doesn't spike her hair. I will look lousy in spiked
hair.

"You're getting too close to yourself," Sukey says.

1

"Go do something nice for somebody else and it will get you out of yourself."

"But if I do something nice for somebody else to get me out of myself, aren't I really just doing something nice for me?"

.

So I think, Hey, I've never been down to Aunt Ida's place. Maybe I should go and see Aunt Ida for the last time. She is the oldest in the family. The oldest sister of my grandmother, the first to go gray, the most bent over, the one with the most body parts removed. The one with the most body parts not hers. A metal hip. An artery that's 100 percent polyester. The thinnest, the poorest. The one widowed first. A son in small leather goods a coast away. Broken-down clothes from relatives. The only thing Aunt Ida ever had first was gallstones. The only thing she could ever really call her own.

I dial her number. I know she will be home because she is recovering from her colostomy.

"Hello?"

"Aunt Ida!"

"Who's this?"

"Letty!"

"Letty who?"

"Letty Bogen. Letty Fenster Bogen."

"Who?"

"Ethel Melnick's granddaughter. Millie Fenster's daughter. Sukey Glogower's sister. Randy Bogen's wife."

"Sukey! Darling! How are you?"

MYSTERY SALAD

"Letty."

"Letty! Darling! How's Sukey?"

"Do you feel like a little company?" I ask. This for sure will be the last time. This really feels like *it*. Aunt Ida is eighty-nine and no longer has a large intestine.

"Come for lunch!" Aunt Ida says. "I haven't seen you in a long time, Sukey."

"Letty."

"Bring her too."

■

I have two hours to kill so I wash my hair and finger-dry it and put on make-up so I look like I'm not wearing any and find a bottle of cream sherry for Aunt Ida and before I know it, I am late. So I take a cab down to a neighborhood that has undergone three ethnic transitions since my great-grandparents first settled there. The thought that I have come down here to console myself by finding a human being more miserable than I am is so awful, I have to tell myself I can't help what I think. I have come down here to get myself out of myself and do a good turn. I have come down here to bring cheer and cream sherry to a dying older woman with missing parts and a son in small leather goods.

■

Aunt Ida's apartment is in a flaking five-story brownstone with a shop on the ground floor that sells trusses, bedpans, and orthopedic shoes. I wonder if

3

there's anything in the store she could use. Maybe the cream sherry is enough. So I open the street door and buzz up. Since Aunt Ida lives on the top floor, her button is on the bottom, beneath Chang, Gonzales, and Marmelst—*Marmelstein* if the name tag had more spaces? Aunt Ida's button is the cleanest. So she's having visitors. That's good. Everyone is coming to see Aunt Ida for the last time. Suddenly I realize I should have brought food. Aunt Ida has no money. Aunt Ida can't go out. Aunt Ida is starving. I despise myself for not thinking of it. Food! The money I spent on taking a cab down here could have kept Aunt Ida in mashed bananas and Beech-Nut Turkey Rice Dinners for a week.

Aunt Ida doesn't answer my buzz, so I hit Chang, Gonzales, and Marmelst, and pretty soon I am in. The walls of the entryway are tiled in yellow, and like all small dark places in the city—the phone booths, service elevators, even the back seats of cabs—it smells like men's piss. Sometimes I think that if I didn't know that smell was men's piss—if it was, say, the smell of a flower—I'd like it.

I start up the stairs, trying to balance myself. There is no banister and the walls lean in so the higher you go, the harder your body presses into them. They are mustard-colored stucco covered in grease. How could my family let Aunt Ida live like this?

I bang on the door and finally shout, "It's me, Aunt Ida, Letty! Let me in!"

Nothing.

I bang harder. "Anybody home?" I shout. Maybe the excitement from my buzzing did her in.

4

Then a police bolt jolts out of the floor. A lock unclicks. A wary Island woman probes me through the gap.

"Who is it, Catherine?" I hear Aunt Ida holler.

"I'm her niece," I say conspiratorially, as if to say, You know how the old are. "She's expecting me."

"She says she's your niece." Catherine hollers back.

Silence.

"Tell her it's Letty Fenster Bogen, please," I say.

Catherine opens the door, keeping her body behind it and, quite suddenly, I am plunged into my youth. Here is the coffee table with the peeling gold-leaf legs that graced my mother's living room when I was growing up, the floor lamp from my grandmother's with the inverted green leather shade that only provided light for the ceiling, the pink convertible sofa that was considered by three generations to be my mother's single most serious consumer error, and the red-and-blue Oriental rug we gave away when we gave away the dog that ruined it.

"Get my niece a chair, Caroline," Aunt Ida says, coming out of the bedroom.

It looks like there's no bulge where the bag is.

"You know what they did to me?" Aunt Ida grabs my arm.

"I can't believe how good you look, Aunt Ida," I say. For the first time, I have to bend down to kiss her. This latest round with the doctors has shaved inches off her height.

"My hair," Aunt Ida says. "You like my hair?"

"How do you do it?" I marvel. Her hair does, in fact, look perfect. "I mean, really."

"Come," she nudges. "I made lunch."

"Aunt Ida! You're supposed to be taking it easy!"

"I didn't do it. Cynthia did it." She nods to Cynthia and Cynthia beams and twists her calves around each other.

My father's old collapsible bridge table is covered with Aunt Fay's green felt canasta cloth. Bright pink cut grapefruits lie like jewels on Uncle Harry's first wife's gilt-edged service plates. Aunt Ida is using Grandma's everyday flatware. I realize I have not seen grapefruit spoons since my grandmother died.

I am struck with the notion that nobody will ever take this trouble for me again, that the last time I will see Aunt Ida is also the last time I will see grapefruit spoons.

"Here's some sherry," I tell Aunt Ida. "You always loved cream sherry."

Aunt Ida opens her mouth and nothing comes out. Then, "Cinderella!" she blurts. "The sherry glasses!"

Cinderella brings, oh my God! Grandpa's silver-rimmed sherry glasses, the ones that he used at his Thursday night pinochle game. I am overcome. I wonder if she also has his wall-size radio with the steering wheel channel selector I used to talk to God on.

Aunt Ida pours half glasses and we clink.

"To health and happiness," she says, and I search her eyes for a double entendre. Does she mean for me? For her? For us?

"So tell me, Sukey," she sighs, "what's new?"

MYSTERY SALAD

Since I haven't seen Aunt Ida in over a year, I don't know whether to tell her that the cleaner lost my favorite blouse yesterday or that actually I'm Letty, not my sister Sukey. What's new? always throws me. Where to start? What's important? How to begin?

"Sukey sends her love," I say.

"Eat!" Aunt Ida is not happy with the progress I am making. In my family, if you haven't ravaged a grapefruit, you haven't enjoyed it. I wonder how many food stamps Aunt Ida sacrificed for an Indian River grapefruit. If it would make her happy, I'd take the zest home for baking and use the oil in the skin for scenting soap.

"So what do you think of my robe?" Aunt Ida asks, waving a bony hand over the dishes, signaling Cinderella.

Cinderella clears.

"You may bring the main course now, Graziela," Aunt Ida tells her.

I say, "Nobody ever wore clothes like you, Aunt Ida. I mean that." The robe is Bermuda blue, Aunt Ida's color, ruffled at the neck and down the front. It stands away from her like clown pants.

Graziela sets the salad down. It is chopped beyond recognition, molded in the center of Aunt Fay's vegetable platter. Aunt Ida dismisses Graziela and serves with authority. It occurs to me that in many ways, Aunt Ida's never had it so good. Full-time help, a new robe. Where did she get this wonderful food?

"You know who sent me this robe?"

"My mother," I guess.

7

"Who?" Aunt Ida says.

"Millie Fenster."

"Norman sent me this robe. Norman! Can you imagine? All the way from California! Such a son I have! Nobody, *nobody* has a son like me!"

She drops some salad on my plate.

"Norman loves you," I say, taking a taste.

"I'm the luckiest woman in the world," Aunt Ida says. "You like the salad?"

"Ummm," I say. It is quite tasty. "What's in it?"

"Guess!" Aunt Ida's blue eyes light up.

"Well, the orange stuff is carrots."

"Carrots, Gracie!" she calls to her companion. "Go on!"

"Chicken?"

"No!"

"Mayonnaise?"

"Hah!"

"Tuna?"

"Hah! Tuna, Stacy! Hah! Hah!"

"I give up," I say, holding my plate up for a second helping. It's unbelievably good.

"Then you'll never know, will you?"

Oh God. Oh no. It's dog food. It must be dog food. How could she afford anything else?

"Eat!" Aunt Ida encourages me. "It's good for you."

"Please tell me what's in it, Aunt Ida."

"And let you steal my recipe? Fat chance."

Aunt Ida takes a bite and chews it with her front teeth.

"Did it come in a can?" I ask.

MYSTERY SALAD

"I made this recipe up from scratch," Aunt Ida says. "You could never duplicate it even if I gave you the recipe. There is a possibility that even I will never be able to duplicate it. Right, Stephanie?"

"Right, Mrs. Stavin." Stephanie nods.

"Only Selena and I know what went into this salad. Only Selena and I will ever know. Now eat. Don't waste."

I feel like eating Aunt Ida's mystery salad is the last kind thing I will ever be able to do for her. Wait till Sukey hears I ate dog food.

"What's in it, Selena?" I ask, turning in my seat. Selena stands behind me so Aunt Ida can catch her eye.

"Don't you tell her, Sabena. I mean it," Aunt Ida says.

"Aw, come on, Sabena. You can tell me."

I can't believe, with everything my family's done for her, Aunt Ida won't give me the recipe.

"No!" Aunt Ida rises out of her seat and shouts.

Since I don't want to be responsible for giving Aunt Ida her last heart attack, I retreat. I can't believe she would make such a big deal about it. What am I going to do? Sell the recipe for a billion dollars to *Family Circle*? She's got the best son in the world, the best robe in the world, does she need the best salad recipe in the world too?

A homemade chocolate cake appears. It is so light, you can see air through it. Light and lofty, almost quivering on . . . what? My old cake stand! How did Aunt Ida get my old cake stand? When was the last time I saw that cake stand? I used to love that cake stand.

"My Norman calls me every week. He can't wait to talk to me," Aunt Ida says. "Always he asks me how I am." Aunt Ida glows. "Always, he says 'Love ya, Mom' before he hangs up. 'Love ya, Ma.' Just like that. I am blessed. You know that?"

"You were a wonderful mother, Aunt Ida. Everybody knows how you fed him heavy cream in his cereal when he was a boy."

"In his cereal! I let him drink it from the bottle."

"Well, a boy doesn't forget that, Aunt Ida."

"I want you to take a piece of cake home. Serena, please. A Ziploc."

Aunt Ida slips a sliver into the bag.

"Could I have another piece for my husband?" I ask.

"Who's this one for?" She waves the Ziploc.

"I thought we could each have a piece for dessert tonight," I say.

Aunt Ida stands up. She sticks the knife in the Ziploc and hacks the cake in half. She looks at me with less than love. I see I have overstepped the line. I stare back at her, trying to memorize her.

"Hey, Aunt Ida," I say, "remember the time at Grandma's you taught me how to roll bread balls on the tablecloth and make my finger feel dead?"

"That's the most disgusting thing I ever heard," she says, waving Aunt Bessie's cake knife at my heart.

I walk to Aunt Ida's side of the table, and push her arm away like a turnstile. I hug her to me. Aunt

MYSTERY SALAD

Ida's breasts do not come between us. I feel nothing but billowing air as I try hugging her tighter, getting closer and closer, waiting to feel the pressure of her colostomy bag against my hip. Aunt Ida smells as sweet as the talc her sister, my grandmother, used to keep on top of the toilet tank.

Aunt Ida pushes me back.

"Sabrina, help me to bed. I'm a little tired."

"I'll help you."

"No. I want Sabrina."

Sabrina offers Aunt Ida her arm and then braces Aunt Ida around the back with her other arm. They walk, locked like ice skaters, into the bedroom.

I pick a crumb off the cake stand and carry the crumb into the kitchen. I open the cabinet door beneath the sink. I tip the garbage pail toward me. It smells medicinal. A few orange and gray carrot scrapings are stuck to the plastic liner bag.

Sabrina comes out of the bedroom looking distracted.

"May I go in and say good-bye?" I ask. Good-bye forever?

"She says to tell you she is resting," Sabrina says. "And to thank you for coming."

"What, exactly, is your name?" I ask Sabrina, adjusting my shoulder bag.

"Elvita," she says, opening the door.

I start to slide out. "And what," I say, as if it's an afterthought, "was in that salad, actually, Elvita?"

"Tofu, honey," she says, closing the door behind me.

Tofu!

Of course!
No.
Wait.
Tofu, *honey?*
Tofu *and* honey?
Or tofu, *honey* as in *dear?*
Or was it tofu, *honky?*

∎

I call my sister to tell her Aunt Ida's on her last leg.

"She's down to one?" my sister Sukey says.

I take a long shot and ask my sister when she gave Aunt Ida my old cake stand.

"You only like that cake stand because somebody else has it," Sukey says.

I tell her about the recipe, how Aunt Ida wouldn't give it to me.

"That's right," my sister Sukey says. "Keep asking people for something. Keep giving them the chance to say no."

"Are you telling me I set myself up? Is that what you're telling me? You think I set myself up?"

"No," my sister Sukey says. "And Liz Taylor never had a face-lift."

THE MIAMI DOLPHINS

L eft *after* the Coppertone sign," Ma says. "We almost missed our turn!"

Suddenly we're on a dirt road, bouncing along. Two hours we're in the car looking for my birthday present.

"*Now* right," Ma says.

There are wild trees on one side. On the other, chicken wire wrapped around the kind of electrical plant that would look at home in *Bride of Frankenstein*. I see a sign. Dad screeches into Betty's Home of the Dolphins.

"Are you the Glassmans?" A woman in a faded bikini leans into the car window. "Where the hell have you been?"

I look around. There are His and Hers Port-O-Sans, a blue-gray shanty with a hand-lettered OFFICE sign above the doorway, and in the water, concrete pens, the kind you'd see in a fish hatchery only bigger.

"What's the story?" I ask them.

They put their arms around each other's waists and start singing "Happy Birthday to You." While they're singing, they point to the pens. "The Miami Dolphins," they say. "You're going to swim with the Miami Dolphins."

I walk over to the water and look down. Nothing's there. The water looks black.

"I'm Betty." The woman pats her sternum. "You people almost missed orientation."

Betty has sun-bleached hair and leathery skin. Her body looks like a lifetime of hard work. I take her to be in her fifties even though she could be thirty or seventy. She motions for us to sit at a picnic table with an elderly couple, a skinny boy, and a fat girl. The old man keeps slapping his legs as if bugs are around only they aren't. The little girl is wearing a bathing suit with pieces cut out of the sides and her fat overlaps the holes. The boy wears madras Bermudas with suspenders and Ray-Bans, a cool dude. The girl looks scared. The boy looks angry. The grandfather looks annoyed. The grandmother looks like she's ready to take notes. She's leaning forward. You can tell she loved school.

"Swimming with the dolphins is therapeutic," Betty begins. "Autistic kids come here to swim. Psychologists send their patients to Betty's Home of the Dolphins all the time."

"I never knew that," the grandma says. "Why is that?"

"For the autistic," Betty explains, "they're hoping to trigger an emotional response. For groups, they're looking for a shared experience to compare reactions." Betty looks around to see if there are any more questions. "The cetacean group," she continues, "includes whales, dolphins, and porpoises."

The grandma raises her hand. "Are these dolphins Flipper?" she asks.

Betty nods and tells us these are *Tursiops truncatus,* Atlantic bottle-nosed dolphins.

I scan the pens looking for one.

"Carl," the grandma taps the grandpa's hand. "Didn't we have these for dinner last night?"

"The dolphin you eat is a fish not a mammal," Betty explains. Then she tells us how dolphins echolocate from their foreheads and their lower jaws.

"I love this," I mouth to my parents, who have been watching for a reaction. "Thank you."

My mind flashes briefly to other presents they have given me: a massage that was a series of drill noogies, a one-year membership in The Fad-of-the-Month Club, kayak lessons, an hour with a career counselor, one month of liquid diet.

"Dolphins can tell if you have a pacemaker," Betty is saying, "and what your blood pressure is. They can tell if you're pregnant. Or if you have to take a dump."

I check Ma on the word "dump." She is frowning.

"They can read right through our bodies," Betty continues. "They can even pick up fetal heartbeats. They have long wave and short wave and they use it to tell the size of something, its density, and to check out the terrain. They use it to find food too. Dolphins have no sense of smell. But they can taste. And they make love every day. Dolphins are the only animals who have sex for fun besides humans."

15

Ma raises her hand. "What about swans?" she says.

Betty doesn't answer. She's looking at the boy. He's rocking sideways on the picnic bench. He looks like he's about to burst.

"I think it's mean you make the dolphins work," he says. "There's no way I'm going."

"Oh yes you are," his grandma says.

Betty starts handing out snorkels, masks, and flippers.

"This is cruelty to animals," the boy protests. "Dolphins don't want to take humans for rides. You make them."

"The dolphins are free to leave anytime they want." Betty points to the canal that leads from the pens to the Atlantic. "We don't have any gates here. The dolphins can leave anytime they want to. But they don't. The dolphins always come back. Now, do you think they'd do that if they were unhappy?"

"Right," the boy says, glaring at Betty over his Ray-Bans. "You feed them, don't you?"

"Of course we do," Betty says. "But they're rewarded whether they do their work or not."

"Jason!" the grandma snaps. "Do you have to ruin it for everybody?"

"We've already paid for you," the grandfather says. "You have to go."

"Forget it." The boy parks his elbows on the picnic table. "I'm not going and you can't make me."

"I can't refund your money," Betty says. "We reserved a place for him."

"I'll pay for it myself. I have enough. I'll pay you not to go."

"Well why don't you go in, Carl?" The grandma turns to the grandpa. "You love to swim."

The little girl runs over to her grandpa. "Please, Grandpa," she says. "I'm scared. I don't want to go in alone."

"This lady is going in with you, Tiffany." The grandpa points to me.

"My daughter cannot be legally responsible for her," Ma says. "My daughter will not take legal responsibility."

"I'm not going in," Tiffany says, and crosses her arms over her chest. The grandpa says, "Jesus Christ!" then pries off his sandals and starts tugging at his socks. Betty tells us to take off all our rings. "Their skin is so sensitive," she says. "Abrasion from a ring gives them excruciating pain." She demonstrates how to latch onto a fin. She holds her hands straight out, palms flat. "Pretend you're doing the breast stroke," she says. "Grab it thumb down." I pretend I'm doing the breast stroke and grab air with my thumbs down.

Ma nudges Dad. Quick he takes a picture.

"You'll each get two rides up front," Betty says. "Then you'll have a play time. At the end, you'll each get one more ride. We do that to make sure everybody has *some* time with the dolphins. Sometimes they pick favorites. No one knows why. They'll ignore one person and they won't leave somebody else alone."

17

The grandma raises her hand. "Is it true a dolphin can kill a shark?" she asks.

Betty nods as she helps Tiffany with her mask. "They hammer sharks in the gills with their noses," she says.

"Who is the natural enemy of the dolphin then," the grandma asks.

"Man," says Betty. "Tuna fishermen. The dolphins get caught in their nets and suffocate. If you ever saw what comes up in a tuna fisherman's net, you'd never eat Chicken of the Sea again. It's enough to break your heart."

"Are you happy?" Ma asks me.

"This is the best present you've ever given me," I tell her.

"See?" she nods to Dad.

"Sh-h-h-h," he says as Betty starts telling us what to expect underwater.

"You'll hear clicks," she says. "That's the dolphins checking you out. They love knees. Human knees from the back resemble the dolphins' sexual organs. Sometimes they'll come and put their mouths around your knees. If you don't like it, just swim away. If you feel something coil up your leg, don't be afraid. That means the male likes you a lot. It means he's attracted to you. Here at Betty's Home of the Dolphins we call that 'The Sea Snake.' "

"Jesus," Dad says under his breath.

"Don't let them do that to you, honey," Ma says.

∎

THE MIAMI DOLPHINS

The grandpa, Tiffany, and I slide down to a small dock in the water. We are wearing our flippers, masks, and snorkels. The three of us look like a catalog picture for what sizes snorkel equipment comes in.

"Smile!" Dad yells down at me. He takes my picture.

Betty stands above us on dry land. She makes a whistling sound with her nose. Suddenly, the water moves. Three waves approach the dock we're standing on. These waves get bigger and come close to each other. When they are right at the dock, the waves break and dolphins rise out of them, rearing backward on their tails. They are sleek as chrome. They open their mouths and chirp. It's a loud, flat sound with no range. Two are big, one's little.

"Sparky! Happy! Mike!" Betty introduces us. The dolphins chirp once more then sink back into the water.

"Forget it. I'm not going," Tiffany says.

"Oh yes you are," her grandpa says.

Betty tells us that dolphins smile whether they are happy or not. "Don't reach out to pet them," she warns us. "If they want you to pet them, they'll let you know. You wouldn't want to be petted by strangers, would you? Dolphins know who they like."

Betty tells us to get in the water and swim to the far side of the pen. That's where the dolphins will pick us up. She tells Tiffany to go in first. Tiffany goes in all right but once her head gets wet, she starts thrashing and coughing.

"I can't do it," she cries. "I can't do it!"

ALL IT TAKES

Betty kneels on the dock and reminds Tiffany how to do it.

"Just bite down and breathe," she says, adjusting Tiffany's mouthpiece. Betty has a calm animal trainer's way about her. You get the feeling she doesn't mind doing the same thing over and over, reducing it always to its simplest form. She shows the little girl how to spit in her mask to keep the glass clear.

"I can't do this," the little girl says in a tired broken way.

"Sure you can," Betty says and the little girl paddles off.

I go in next. I keep telling myself this has to be okay. You never hear of people being killed by dolphins. This is 1989. Elevators get inspected. Businesses are licensed. Lawyers are waiting in the wings.

The water is warm. "Got it!" Dad shouts from behind the camera as I swim toward the little girl.

Then her grandfather falls off the deck backward. He's watched too many re-runs of "Sea Hunt." You don't go in backward with a snorkel. Even I know that. He surfaces with his mask under his chin. He swims over to where Tiffany and I are lined up.

"Here." I motion him in front of me. "You want to be next to Tiffany?"

"Wave!" Dad shouts. I wave, then stick my head in the water. I can't see any dolphins. The water is green with yellow dust all through it. When I surface, the little girl is being towed by Sparky, the littlest dolphin. Her head is in the water. She looks like she knows what she's doing. But when she raises her head, her mask is filled with water, and she's crying and choking.

Betty leans down. She talks to the little girl and fixes her mask.

The grandfather turns to me. "I'm next," he says. "God help me."

I check underwater again to see if I can see the dolphin coming for him. Then I get distracted by a sea anemone doing the hula on the bottom of the pen. When I look back, the little girl and her grandpa are swimming toward me.

I don't know what's going on. I don't know what to expect. I don't know what the dolphin is making of my rapidly beating heart. Maybe it thinks I'm an enemy. Something takes me over that must be a kind of REM sleep for the awake. I'm conscious but it feels like a dream. My eyes are working but I'm not seeing. My ears are okay, but I can't hear. The water breaks beside me. A gray mass is there. It's a warm wet gray. It's hard to believe anything alive could be so perfect. The mass turns. The mass is a head. It looks at me with an eye bigger than a cow's and much, much more intelligent.

"Got it," Dad shouts. "Smile!"

I look it straight back in the eye. Now I understand why Shirley MacLaine thinks we were all animals once or vice versa. The dolphin is somehow human. He looks like he can read my mind. It's as if he knows something about me I don't know. In case he is reading my mind, I think nice dolphin thoughts. Pretty dolphin, I think. Smart. You're the best thing in the sea.

ALL IT TAKES

You're the King of the Sea, I think, then excuse myself for the tunalike reference. I want this dolphin to like me. I want us to be friends. I'm not going to force myself on you, I think. Anything you want is fine with me. You're the boss. How much do you weigh?

"He's waiting for you," Betty yells, making a megaphone out of her hands.

The dolphin disappears then surfaces again. He wags his fin an inch from my right arm.

I think "breast stroke" and grab it thumb down. He takes off immediately and we're knifing through the water. I'm going the fastest I've ever gone in the water. Much faster. We're leaving a wake. I'm in an element I don't belong in with something that makes me fit. I am swimming like a dolphin, slicing through the water. This dolphin is making me a dolphin. This is the best moment of my life. I always want to remember this. For twenty seconds, I'm a dolphin. He drops me off at the dock and disappears.

•

The three of us line up in the same order again. We tread water, curling our fingers through a wire fence. The little girl goes, then her grandpa, then me. My plan is to keep my head underwater this time and breathe through the snorkel to make myself even more like a dolphin. But when I do, it's a little less good than it was the first time. Maybe it's because I'm anticipating how great it's going to be. That's what happens with expectations. It's fine. It's wonderful. But it's just fun.

THE MIAMI DOLPHINS

■

"Free time!" Betty shouts, and we all swim to the middle of the pen. The dolphins have disappeared. Maybe they've gone out to sea.

"You were wonderful!" Ma shouts, and I wave to the camera.

"We got everything!" Dad says.

Just then, all three dolphins surface around the little girl and start nudging her with their noses. She screams through her snorkel then rips it off.

Betty stands on the dock and shouts. "They're just being friendly! They like you! They want to take you for a ride! Grab one!"

All three wiggle their fins and the little girl takes one. It's Sparky's. The two big dolphins follow Sparky and the little girl like an escort. She keeps coughing and going under, but she doesn't let the dolphin go.

When the dolphins go past us, her grandfather tries to grab a fin. "Son of a bitch" comes out of his snorkel. We watch the dolphins court Tiffany.

I swim over to Betty. "What's the story," I say.

"Well," she answers, "they really like her. They often like the smallest person best."

The grandfather comes over and complains. "I'm paying you so I can swim with the dolphins," he says.

"You know what you can do?" Betty says. "Try doing something funny underwater. Be a clown. They love that. They'll come if you amuse them."

So I surface dive and snap my fingers underwater. I pound my stomach and burp into my snorkel. When I resurface, the little girl is still being towed in circles by Sparky, followed by the other two dolphins. She's screaming and crying, but she's not letting go. I decide to try humming underwater. I do "It's Cherry Pink and Apple Blossom White" from the movie *Underwater*. I try to imitate their faint clicking sounds. But no matter what I do, the dolphins won't come. I see some motion underwater and swim toward it. The grandfather is doing the Charleston on the bottom of the pen and hitting himself in the head. When I surface, the little girl is screaming, "I can't do it!" but she's still holding on. Betty is yelling to her, "Sparky loves you!"

I try to figure out what the dolphins have against me. Is it the sausage I ate this morning? What makes me undesirable to a dolphin? I could lose a little weight. I've had anxiety lately. Maybe I'm ovulating. I go under again and try to think of what a clown would do. I decide to walk into a wall. Just as I get up to the wall of the pen, I feel something wrap around my leg. It's soft and gentle. I'm facing the wall of the pen and something is wrapping itself up and around my leg. I panic and pull away. When I turn, nothing is there.

"Free time is over!" Betty shouts. We line up again. The dolphins take us each for a ride and then it's over.

"I got a lot of good shots," Dad says, handing me a towel.

"I think we should get our money back," Ma says. "Those dolphins obviously don't like adults."

"Don't," I say. "This was the best present you ever gave me. I loved it. I swear."

THE MIAMI DOLPHINS

But no matter what I say, my parents will be disappointed. They will be disappointed because they think I am. The truth is, I am. I would have liked more dolphin rides. I would have liked the dolphins to like me.

As we head for the car, I hear the skinny boy tell his sister, "I'm going to report you to the ASPCA."

■

In the car, we try to make our minds up about dinner. The choice is Crabs R Us, Flynn's Dixie Ribs, or Grilled Anything. I vote for Grilled Anything because I want to see what things can be grilled I never dreamed of. Ma and Dad are not talking in the front of the car. I explain to them how much I loved the present, but they will not be consoled. Their daughter has been rejected by dolphins and in the back of their minds, they're wondering why. Is there something wrong with their daughter? Is it something she did? It occurs to me then that even though they've retired to Boca Raton, even though their lives are completely different, nothing has changed. No matter what happens to me, no matter what I do, their joy in me peaked years ago. The best moment they ever had with me has come and gone. It is unduplicatable. It can never happen again. I can never again be a seven-year-old on talent night at Kropnick's Kozy Kabins in the Catskills. I can never again be their tatahlah, their bubahlah, their laban-on-the-keppahlah singing "She's Too Fat for Me" with a back drop of mountains on a stage lit by candles in jelly jars. I can never again afford my parents the opportunity of being elbowed by near strangers saying, "Is she something? Is she delicious? Could you eat her up?"

"No matter what you think, I loved it," I say.

"I knew she'd hate it," Dad says to Ma.

"We tried to please her." Ma shakes her head.

"We tried to do something out of the ordinary and we failed," Dad says.

"It's enough to break your heart, Dave."

BLUE
LIGHT

On my way uptown to Billy's, I stop by Macy's. The 7:00 A.M. news said Macy's is getting a delivery of six hundred Squaw Babies before noon. My daughter Zoe has never been attached to a doll. She likes to destroy books. It puzzles us, this book ripping. Ed and I have such reverence for our books. We love them all. The ones on the shelves. The ones that spill onto chairs, pile up on the coffee table, dodder on the floor. Often we discuss who Zoe takes after. On what chromosome is book ripping found? Whose side of the family? Why us?

While Ed does not believe in turning children into consumers, he thinks Squaw Baby might help. Squaw Baby is the first doll Zoe has ever asked for, and if she can learn to love a doll, Ed thinks she can learn to love books. Ed says once Zoe learns to love, we can teach her how to use that love on anything. He says application follows feeling. So I go to Macy's before Billy's where I find myself propelled by a human wave, buoyed by mothers, my toes barely grazing the escalator grate.

There are men there too. Men, florid and intense, overcoats flying, fighting their way to the Squaw Baby display. I get my hand on one. I am actually feeling the box. I try to grip the cardboard, fingers scrambling like a rock climber. But the box disappears. The crowd thins. The last Squaw Baby is gone.

"I was so close," I tell Billy at the Four Brothers. We have just made love. "I almost had a Squaw Baby in my hand."

"Want to see a girl who looks just like Woody Allen?" he says.

"Where?" I ask, looking around the coffee shop.

"Okay, want to see a girl who looks just like Woody Allen *blond*?"

Now I see the girl. Same channels down the sides of her face. Same baffled eyebrows. Most of all, same lips, lips that look tucked under like the hem of a skirt.

■

Billy makes me see things I never would have noticed. He is a painter. To support his painting, he ghostwrites Civil War books. To support ghostwriting Civil War books, he is superintendent in a brownstone in Hell's Kitchen. Technically, the Civil War stuff isn't subsidized by being a super. Being a super allows Billy to live rent-free, which then allows him to write the Civil War stuff to support his painting.

In addition to making me see things I never would have seen, Billy has given me whole new things to think about. Chickamauga. Flushometers. Moxley Sor-

rel. Bastard pipes. And General Pierre Gustave Toutant
Beauregard.

One of his favorite things to do when the two of us
are alone on his bed on the floor with his chin resting
on the top of my head as if our pieces were designed
like a puzzle to fit together perfectly, lying that way, so
close, one of Billy's favorite things to do is whisper
snappy biographies of himself. He composes them in
flashes of sotto voce brilliance. I like the ones that I
am in best. He imagines, long after his death, what
perceptive biographers will make of his work.

*"Quote. While historians have argued that Billy Ogg's
somber palette is attributed to retinitis pigmentosa, new
findings reveal that his subterranean studio offered little
light. Unquote."*

*"Quote. Billy Ogg's drift in the late eighties to fuzzy
penumbrae is directly attributed to the lighting in his
studio. Ogg worked only with neon light and at night.
Unquote."*

*"Quote. The noted Civil War buff, Billy Ogg, was a
painter by night and a plumber during the day. Kitty
Haber posed for many of his nudes. He was particularly
enchanted by her fecund hips. Unquote."*

The neon lighting is the EVRO from a Chevrolet
dealer sign in the Bronx. It makes everything bluish.
Red is purple. Yellow is green. Green is blue-green.
Blue, blue-blue. The light is such a presence, I am

always surprised I cannot feel it, scoop it up in my hand and take it with me. Put some in my handbag to take home for Zoe. Snap some in my parka and, when everyone is asleep at night, open the pocket under the covers and let the blue light swarm around Ed's bare and scratchy ankles.

How strange Billy always looks to me in the light of the Four Brothers. I prefer making coffee in his studio. There the coffee is really black. Black and blue-black. There I don't have to worry if I will be seen with Billy even though I could easily explain that I was interviewing him for my postmodern series, *Beauty Counts*. Still, I prefer the peace of the blue EVRO, so scrupulously clean. No dust hairs dull its glow.

•

I try to see Billy only once every two weeks. I try and most of the time I am successful. Knowing I can see Billy anytime, that he is always there writing, painting, or fixing a pipe, is solace to me. Knowing he is always there keeps me from needing to see him too much. In the four months since we started, he has never not been there when I knocked. I worry that one day he will not be there. I am also afraid that if I see Billy more, it will jeopardize things with Ed. I don't want to do that. Ed loves me more than I've ever been loved. Ed loves me much more than Billy does. And Ed loves me more than I love Billy. So it makes sense to me to stick with Ed. And, of course, there is Zoe.

My goal is to not want Billy. But since that seems impossible now, I will settle for not letting Billy into the rest of my life. I will keep Billy and Ed separate, blue light from clear light, until I have the power not to visit Billy anymore. He always looks surprised when he opens the door, framed in blue light, holding his paintbrush, wrench, or Liquid Paper, his crunchy yellow hair shining like green metal. Whatever he is holding he puts down and holds me. And everytime, after I have left Billy, after Zoe and Ed are definitely sleeping, I try to reconstruct the day and see who pulled away first. I close my eyes and see Billy in the doorway, no more a part of the real world than blue light. And I think:

"*Quote. Kitty Haber, best remembered for* Making Chaos Out of Order *and* The Propriety of Appropriation, *was rumored to have been the inspiration of Billy Ogg. In lieu of flowers, please send contributions to Yale College, School of Fine Arts. Unquote.*"

I can find Billy's mouth with my eyes closed. I never have to rout for it. He never tires of calling me his pre-Raphaelite. And after we make love (we always make love first, we try sometimes to talk or have coffee or paint first, but so far we can't), after we make love, Billy likes to paint me while I am lying on the bed and he is hovering on a ladder. He paints me, looking down, from above. A favorite technique is painting the intricate folds of blue sheet around me leaving me out, my form defined by the places sheet is missing, negative space. I am defined by what isn't me.

31

ALL IT TAKES

"Quote. To protect the reputation of his beloved Kitty, who was married to a world-famous analyst, Ogg painted only around her, never her. Unquote."

"How will anyone ever know I'm your muse if you never paint my face?" I ask Billy, laughing.

"Quote. The unpublished diaries of Kitty Haber, graciously offered to scholars by Mrs. Haber's daughter Zoe, while making no direct mention of Ogg, refer to a blue light source that could only be Ogg's. Unquote."

"But I don't keep a diary," I say.

"Quote. The lyrical proportion of hips to hair, the flamboyantly rococo curve of the fingers, the uninterrupted taper of thigh to ankle, was unique to a frequent guest of Ogg's, Kitty Haber, according to the proprietors of the Four Brothers Coffee Shop on West 44th Street. Unquote."

I laugh and bloat with happiness. Billy drips a drop of paint on me. It lands in a perfect blue circle on the cusp of my knee. Billy climbs down and wipes me clean and I want him so powerlessly that I feel weepy. He wants me too. With him we always want each other the same. For my birthday, he painted a line drawing of me superimposed on his own body in food dye.

Although I know this really happened, my dreams have more reality. So I asked him once, "Billy, did you really paint me on you? Did I dream that?" And he held his palms out from his hips, where his drawing had gone off the board.

•

At home I reheat the pot roast and stir white horseradish into a jar of Mott's Apple Sauce.

Ed comes through the door with a package under his arm. Zoe looks up from the book she is slicing. I shiver from the cold Ed carries on his coat.

"Smells good," he says, sniffing the air. He kisses me appreciatively. "Pot roast?"

"It's better the second time around," I say because A, it's true and B, there's no time to cook on the days I visit Billy.

Ed hangs up his coat and squats on the floor next to Zoe. He always speaks to her eye to eye. After ten hours of analyzing patients who look only at the ceiling, Ed is rigorous about eye contact.

"What are you doing to your book?" Ed asks kindly, flexing his nose to push up his glasses.

"It's going to be a tutu." Zoe holds the shredded book up proudly. "I'm going to dance in it."

"Before or after you play with Squaw Baby?" Ed hands Zoe the box. I put my spoon down and come over. Zoe unwraps the package, stealing looks at Ed. Then she raises the lumpy rubber face to her lips and murmurs:

"I'm going to love you," she says. "I'm going to talk to you every day. You are my special child."

Zoe removes the doll from its papoose. She turns
Squaw Baby over and examines her with thoroughness
and grace.

"I'm going to take good care of Squaw Baby," Zoe
tells Ed. "I'm her mother. Want to play Nintendo?" she
says to the doll.

■

At dinner Zoe sets a place for Squaw Baby. A
birth certificate in the box says its name is Little Deer.
Zoe cuts tiny pieces of pot roast for Little Deer, who
sits on two telephone books and stares at Ed's tie clasp
over the rim of her papoose.

When Zoe and Little Deer are tucked into bed and
the lights are out, when we hear big distances between
Zoe's murmurs, Ed tells me he got the doll at Macy's.

"How?" I ask. "I was there. You were there?"

As it turns out, Ed was there when I was there. I
try to ignore the feeling that he saw me without my
seeing him. That the hand reaching from behind me to
steal my Squaw Baby might have been his. That he
might have followed me out of the store, suspicious
because every two weeks he gets the same meal two
nights in a row. That he might have tracked me in the
Subaru to Billy's, then followed us to the Four Brothers, then back to Billy's.

"I found out why they call them Squaw Babies
today," Ed says, sipping coffee from a mug he bought
stamped DADDY.

"Tell me," I say with enthusiasm. I curl up by
his feet while he sits in the best chair. "Tell me.

I was wondering how the Squaw Baby thing got started."

"When children asked where they came from years ago, parents would say, 'I got you from the Indians.' "

"Really?" I say, then add because I know he will enjoy it, "My parents always told me they found me in a garbage can."

Ed brightens. He strokes his Minoan beard. This is just the kind of information he loves. He swoops down on it like an eagle spotting a mouse.

"A garbage can. A garbage can. Well, so, what did you think of that?"

"I didn't believe it."

"You didn't?"

"Never. I knew it couldn't be true."

"How did you know it couldn't be true?"

"Because I would have remembered grapefruit rinds on my shoulders. Remember when garbage was only grapefruit rinds, coffee grinds, and cracked egg shells?"

"What's garbage today?" Ed is still perked up, antennae trembling.

"Aluminum foil, plastic take-out containers, dry-cleaning bags. Crunchy things."

"Ah, yes," Ed says, fondling his mug. "Petrochemicals. Whatever happened to good old-fashioned garbage?"

I realize, quite unexpectedly, that Billy's garbage is old-time garbage. Heavy on paper and rags with a preponderance of grapefruit rinds, coffee grinds, and egg shells. Retro-garbage. All-natural garbage. Biodegradable.

"Should we look in our garbage and see what's in it?" Ed asks.

"I know everything that's in there," I say, leaning my head against his knee. Reflexively, Ed strokes my hair. "I'd say we have eclectic garbage, postmodern, a lot of references in it to classical garbage, yet definitely late eighties. Cuke peels and safety seals. Moldy cantaloupe and the plastic mesh from the onion bag. An empty Ivory Liquid squeeze bottle. Furry cottage cheese."

Ed is impressed.

"All that fuss about a doll with a face like a baked potato," I say.

"Well, she's a consumer now." Ed sounds as if he's losing her. "Maybe it's what she needed."

I let my head lay heavy on his leg. I am tired and comfortable, scared but hopeful.

We sit that way till Zoe calls us.

"Mommy! Daddy! Little Deer's thirsty!"

We stand by Zoe's bed with a glass of ice water. Her brow is lined with concern. She gives Little Deer a sip and asks, "Better?" Little Deer's head wobbles yes. Zoe stretches out her own sips, then hands back the glass. Ed bends down to kiss Zoe one last time, and I see us from above as if I were on a ladder. I see us as small and delicate as a crèche, a modern counterpart to the families you once saw on old *Saturday Evening Post* covers. And I know at that moment that Ed will never appreciate that my hair, when splayed on a pillow, is the exact width of my hips. He will never be high enough to see it, and if he were high enough, he wouldn't notice it. I could, however, tell him that my

36

hair spreads out to the same width as my hips, exactly the same, and he would like to hear that. He would fasten onto it and enjoy it. He would let it disintegrate on the roof of his mouth and smile at it while he drove in the Subaru. He would put it in his pocket and take it out at night and examine it under the covers where, sooner or later, my tapered, freshly shaved ankle finds its way under his.

"How much do you love me?" Zoe asks, holding up her arms for one last hug.

"More than every grain of sand on every beach there ever was."

"Well, I love Little Deer more than every hair on every animal that ever lived."

"Well, I love you a hundred times that," I say, squeezing her wiry body as much as she can take.

"Well, I love Little Deer *infinity* times that." Zoe loosens her grip on my neck. Then "Kiss your granddaughter good night," she says, thrusting the doll at me.

I peck her rubbery cheek.

"You're going to be a good grandma," she says, tucking Little Deer back in. "Tomorrow you can take us shopping."

•

I keep busy in the kitchen until Ed turns off the TV in the bedroom. I make myself a cup of tea and know that if I stay awake out here in the living room for a half hour or so, Ed will be asleep amid the brick walls, mephitic toads, and mothers shaped like

canned hams that people his dreams. And once he
is asleep, he will not wake himself. Dreaming, to
Ed, is a sacred activity. That's the kind of thing you
know when you've been married long as I have.

THE HIGH-
BOUNCING LOVER

Dooley is determined not to open her eyes until she is sure which way her body is pointing. Ever since Charlie and Jen moved the house, the perfect house, to the new place, the perfect place, Dooley has had this problem when she visits.

Dooley concentrates and in her mind sees the pine chest of drawers against the salmon floral wallpaper as being at her feet, which means the door is to the left and her head is facing west, provided the night table with the lamp is on the right. Unless her head is turned to the other side, which it feels like it is, and her back is to the door. Dooley panics and opens her eyes. Her head is facing west toward the window. The doorway is to the left, the pine drawers opposite.

Dooley steps into her bathing suit. She pictures Charlie and Jen having coffee downstairs at the old kitchen table she bought for nine dollars at a tag sale. Four years ago, when Jen told Dooley she was so lonely sometimes she called the Eddie Bauer toll-free number just to talk to the down expert, Dooley brought up Charlie. "He's divorced. He's got a son. He's in analysis," she told Jen. "But he's funny. And besides, I can't stand a man once I've had his abortion."

Now every summer Dooley comes to visit, staying one night only in the house that used to be hers. She comes because she still loves the house and because she's curious about Charlie and Jen. Dooley comes to see how they are getting along. She comes to reassure herself that she has not made a mistake, passing Charlie to Jen. Why, she wonders, couldn't I have loved him as much as I love this house?

The house is a scrupulously restored Cape with weathered gray shingles and white trim. Charlie and Jen decided to move it when a series of asymmetrical houses sprouted in the potato fields surrounding them. They moved the house from the northern fork of Long Island to a more isolated part. But now, standing by the upstairs window, Dooley sees that new houses are going up all around them. Charlie and Jen can't outrun the new houses. They are angular and look as if they were built in sections. Then the sections were put together at random, like a Rubik's Cube in a state of flux. If you could take the angular pieces off and put them on a different way, Dooley thinks, maybe you could turn these new houses into Capes.

•

Charlie watches Dooley and Jen through the kitchen window. Jen in her stone-washed string bikini sits beside Dooley in her black tank suit. They remind him of two disparate things found on a beach. As different as a shark's egg case and a ball of tin foil, or a crab skeleton and a peach pit. Two things that have nothing in common except their proximity. Narrow, rounded Jen's back with a spine like a string of beads. And Dooley, mountainous and spreading, with thighs thicker than his waist, a slab of a woman. He wonders if it takes too little to make him happy because each of these women have satisfied him. There was no gap between Dooley and Jen. Yet they are so different. He loves Jen. He wants to make her happy. But he loves Dooley too. The truth is, he could be happy with either one of them. Maybe I'm just lucky, he tells himself, studying the bones of his tan foot. A lucky man. He flexes his toes till the white cords that run from the base of his toes to his ankle pop. He has perfect feet and knows they are perfect. Dooley used to do magical things to his feet with her hands, things that made him feel young. He looks at his feet and thinks, They are the only things about me that have not aged. Then he makes kirs for the ladies. He makes them his own way. Ice first, then wine, then a slow stream of cassis that settles, unmixed, on the bottom of the glass. He does not stir the kirs, so that after Dooley and Jen sip off the slightly cassised wine, they are left with the slightly wined cassis.

▪

"Want me to start lunch?" Jen asks, picking her drink up in the kitchen. Now it's her turn to watch Charlie from the window. She watches as he sits down next to Dooley facing the water, knees bent, toes up,

41

heels in the sand. As they talk to each other the view of the ocean between their heads disappears. Jen pours Charlie a glass of wine.

"Charlie!" she yells out the window. "Ice?"

"Two cubes!" Dooley answers.

Jen opens the freezer and wonders if Dooley could get Charlie back. Dooley has no trouble getting men. Jen thinks about the day they moved the house. Dooley drove out to watch and Jen watched the men—the electricians, the phone men, the contractors, and the plumbers—watch Dooley. When they'd jacked up the house, when they were ready to drive it down the highway, Dooley barked, "Wait!" While everyone stood by, Dooley climbed back into the house and left a Styrofoam cup of coffee on the kitchen table. "When it's all over, when the house is down, I'm going to pull my chair up and finish that coffee."

The men applauded.

"It won't work," Jen said. "Even if it does work, the coffee will be cold."

But Dooley didn't care if the coffee was cold, and it had worked.

•

"Lunch!" Jen calls, setting platters out on the porch. Jen excuses herself to go upstairs and take her temperature. When she comes downstairs, she shakes her head at Charlie and serves the cold lamb. Jen had grilled a butterfly of lamb the night before. Jen always makes the same menu when guests stay over. Grilled butterfly of lamb, spaghetti with pesto, and tomato salad Saturday. Then Sunday, lunch is always cold grilled butterfly of lamb and the cold spaghetti tossed with the leftover tomatoes. On Saturday night, Jen watches when people help themselves at dinner, calculating. Her eyes dart. Will I have enough for tomorrow? What if Charlie takes seconds? Dooley enjoys her power, when on Saturday night she reaches over to the lamb platter for the third time, pauses, then reaches for another slice of herb bread instead. When the house was Dooley's, Dooley always cooked too much. Dooley thinks a table should look like Thanksgiving at every meal. She thinks guests should have the opportunity to groan, "No! I can't! Not another bite!" Dooley likes big meals with big bowls and big platters heaped with food. Everything sprinkled with handfuls of parsley, dill, or basil from the garden. Pine nuts, capers, Parmesan.

•

"For years I worried I was pregnant," Jen says, furling her spaghetti. "Now I'm worried I'm not."

Dooley looks from Charlie to Jen and back. She tries to piece together what their baby would look like. They both have tight black curly hair, brown eyes, and, in the summer, skin the color of peanut butter. They both have straight noses. They're both thin. They look like brother and sister. Only their smiles seem unrelated. Charlie's is full-lipped and bright, his only lushness. Jen's is thin and jagged, her lips going up and down too many times like the rim of a broken glass.

"But I'm not discouraged," Jen says. "We've only

been trying less than a year. There's a whole nother thing we can try if trying doesn't work."

"Like what?" Dooley asks, genuinely interested.

"Well," Jen hesitates. "There's something Charlie can do. And if that doesn't work, I can try insemination. If insemination doesn't work, I can try *in vitro*."

"That's the dish thing, right?"

"They take eggs from me, then they take sperm from Charlie, then they put them together. Then after they get together, they put them back in me."

"Jen," Dooley says with real feeling. "I hope you won't have to do that."

"Yeah, Jen. I hope you won't," Charlie says as if it's Jen's project, as if he has nothing to do with it.

"Have you tried apple juice?" Dooley remembers something she heard once.

"Where?"

"You *drink* it, Jen." Dooley laughs. Charlie laughs too. But Jen stays serious.

"That's only if you're acidic," her voice wobbles. "That only helps if you're killing the sperm."

"Aw, honey," Charlie rises. "Don't be blue. It'll happen. You'll see."

Jen's head is down. She looks like the kid any kid can make cry.

"Why don't we get married now?" Charlie can't stand seeing anybody sad. He kneels by her chair. "We could get married now if you want. We don't have to wait for a baby."

Jen looks at Dooley. "You really think I'll get pregnant?"

"I really do," Dooley says.

■

After lunch they stand with their toes in the water.

"You know," Dooley says. "you were right to move the house. No one can build on the ocean."

"But look." Charlie points. "Look over there."

Dooley hadn't noticed that one. Now that she sees it, she can't imagine how she missed it. A sharply pitched roof, sketched in two-by-fours, emerges from a grove of scrub pines.

"Come," Charlie says. "Let's visit the neighbors."

They walk across the dunes until they are standing in front of the house.

"Looks like your basic solar-conscious triangle," Dooley says as they study the outline. "But you know what? As long as the roof all goes in the same direction, it won't be too bad. It's when the angles rear up and confront each other, you know, like two dinosaurs fighting? that it's really bad. Then it's a house in conflict. A house that's fighting with itself. Know what I mean?" Dooley looks at them but they stare back and say nothing. She sees they have no idea what she is talking about.

"Come on," Dooley says. "Let's find the front door."

They walk looking down because they don't have shoes on. Charlie helps Dooley and Jen over a mound of dirt and they enter a labyrinth of wood. They explore, sidestepping beer cans and nails. They separate, go their own ways, then meet in the living room. There is an opening between the wood slats for an enormous picture window.

"Oh!" Jen says. "I hope they paint the window trim white. Shiny white. Like a bib for the ocean."

"People who build modern houses don't have moldings around the windows, honey," Charlie says.

"Oh, but don't you think it's nice? Don't you know they'll put a big white sofa there?" Jen points across from the window. "I mean, there's a lot to be said for a modern house."

"What?" Dooley and Charlie say together. Dooley remembers long days of stripping woodwork with Charlie. The thousands of little victories as long strips of layered paint curled off against her chisel. She remembers the special kind of love she and Charlie made when they were physically exhausted. Greedy and determined. Slippery and smelly. She remembers as good as that lovemaking was, he never made a noise, just concentrated like he was stripping wood.

"Well . . ." Jen sounds as if she's looking through her pocketbook for keys. "Well . . . modern houses always have better insulation. When our house was built they didn't know much about insulation."

"Jen," Dooley says. "Do you know what insulation is today? It's thick pink fiberglass batting covered with aluminum foil covered with dry wall filled with rat hair. You can get sarcoid carcinoma from a new house."

"Charlie," Jen ignores Dooley. "Do you think it would help if we did it in a different environment?"

■

Back at the house, Jen comes downstairs. Charlie looks up. She shakes her head.

"Time for Dooley's doggy bag," Jen says, heading for the kitchen.

"Make sure you put some mint in," Charlie calls. "Dooley loves it."

Dooley drops her overnight bag by the front door and thinks about the doggy bag with the leftover leftovers. She thinks about unwrapping the wilted mint in her stingy high-rise kitchen and the bug that will crawl out and make a new home for itself in her apartment. Then she thinks about Jen's body. How it will look with a domed belly and rigid torpedo breasts. She tries to imagine a stressed vein, blue and ropish, pulsing behind Jen's knee. Dooley cannot picture this. What she can picture is Charlie and Jen, dressed in architectonic clothes, strolling down Madison Avenue on a perfect fall Saturday, an exquisite Korean orphan girl between them.

"I guess it's getting to be that time," Jen says, handing Dooley a yellow miniature shopping bag.

"Time for a hat!" Charlie rubs his hands together. "Hat time!"

The three of them walk over to the hat wall and study the hats. There are dozens of hats, hats from the floor to the ceiling, each one hung on its own Shaker peg. Fedoras, crushers, cloches, a Panama, leghorns, plain boaters, political boaters, Dutch boys, porkpies, Wellingtons, a homburg, six bowlers, two Bretons, a slouch, a turban, a collapsible beaver top hat with springs, a fez, a ski mask, gag hats, party hats, golf caps, baby blue tulle Queen Mother hats, a bus driver's hat, a WWI helmet, a pith helmet, a surgeon's hat, two sombreros, a tiara, cowboy hats, a beanie with a propeller on top, a sailor hat, baseball caps, a McDonald's Nehru, a bride's hat with a veil, a pilgrim's hat, a busted wimple.

Hats belong on heads, Dooley thinks. Babies belong in wombs. Houses should stay where they came from. God, she thinks. If you have enough money, maybe you can make anything go anywhere. Maybe reality depends on how much money you have.

•

They face the hat wall. Since Jen started it, many guests bring their own hats. The ones that don't, take whatever hat they want. Before guests leave, they pose with Charlie and Jen and Charlie takes a picture of them, setting the timer, running frantically to make sure he's in it before the timer goes off.

Charlie takes the picture. The three of them sit on the couch waiting for it to develop. They look through the purple Louis Sherry tin full of pictures of guests in hats.

"That's Finkelstein in the sombrero," Charlie says.

"No," Jen squints. "That's Lothar. See the socks?"

"Do you realize," Charlie says, spreading the pictures across six knees, "that every time the Kaprelians come, they wear the same hats?"

"Look at this," Jen nods. "First it's Corinne in the bowler and Barry in the pillbox. Then the next year it's

Corinne in the bowler and Barry in the pillbox again. But wait. The next year, it's *Corinne* in the pillbox and *Barry* in the bowler. Then the next year, it's back to Corinne in the bowler and Barry in the pillbox." Jen looks from Charlie to Dooley. "What do you think?"

"Why, those little devils!" Dooley says. "Those Kaprelians! You know what I think? I think the Kaprelians do that imagining you sitting here on a Sunday afternoon trying to figure out why they do that."

"Do you think it's odd that she mainly wears a man's hat and he mainly wears a woman's?"

"No," Charlie says. "I don't think so. Definitely I'd say no. I'd say the really strange thing is that they always go for the *same* hats. It's not the sex of the hats at all. What do you think, Dools?"

Charlie leans forward, pulling the tail of his knitted maroon shirt out of the back of his bathing trunks. Dooley remembers the island of sparse hair on the base of his spine. He wears the collar of his knitted shirt up. A feeling Dooley has trouble recognizing begins to well up inside her.

"Look," Charlie holds two pictures. "Here's Simon with a John Deere on two years in a row!"

"I don't like hats with words on them," Jen says. "I don't like having to read a hat."

"Look at this." Charlie hands Dooley a photo. "This is what I hate the most. Could you please tell me why people do this?"

The feeling swells inside Dooley. It gets bigger and bigger.

"Charlie, some people think putting a hat on backward is funny. That's all it is," Jen says. "Didn't Jerry Lewis do that?"

"Umpires do. Catchers." Charlie studies the hat wall. "Hey," he says. "We don't have an umpire's hat!"

"We don't have a tricorn either," Jen says. "You know, I understand that Marianne Moore was completely bald under her tricorn. Isn't that interesting? And isn't it interesting how you always associate some people with some hats?"

Dooley feels the feeling about to burst.

"Pillbox!" Charlie shouts.

"Jackie!" Jen shouts back.

"Beanie!"

"Spanky!"

"Gray slouch!"

"George Raft!"

"Turban!"

"Loretta Young!"

"Bzzzzz! Wrong! Sorry!" Charlie says. "Turban is Louise Nevelson."

"Oh? So? What's the difference? They both wore false eyelashes."

Charlie and Jen crack each other up.

"Do false eyelashes go with a turban?" Charlie gasps.

"I once read Loretta Young had special turbans made for her honeymoons so her husbands wouldn't have to see her in curlers."

"But didn't they have to see her in turbans?"

50

THE HIGH-BOUNCING LOVER

Charlie and Jen are holding their sides now, stamping their feet on the floor.

Dooley walks over to the bookshelves. She finds it right away. It's an early paperback edition of *The Great Gatsby* she bought at the firehouse sale for a quarter. She turns to the title page.

Then wear the gold hat, if that will move her;
If you can bounce high, bounce for her too,
Till she cry "Lover, gold-hatted, high-bouncing lover,
I must have you!"

Dooley looks at the hat wall. She slips the book back onto the shelf. Whatever she was about to feel arrives. Dooley lets it flood her. She bathes in it, letting it seep into her pores. It feels good. It feels like the truth. I did the right thing, Dooley thinks. I made the right decision. I never have to wonder again.

Jen closes the Louis Sherry tin. "You know," she says, "every time we add a new picture to the box, it affects all the other pictures. Who else has chosen that hat? What do they have in common? Has that person remained true to a particular hat or has that person varied their hat? You could probably do a scholarly paper on 'Personality and Hat Selection.' Choice of hat says a lot about a person." Jen pulls her Marlene Dietrich low over one eye. "Know vhat I mean, dahlink?"

"I wish Groucho had worn a hat." Charlie flexes his eyebrows and taps an imaginary cigar. "He's the only one I can do."

ALL IT TAKES

■

Together they stand in the driveway and wave good-bye to Dooley, Charlie in his tam-o'-shanter, Jen in her Dietrich. Dooley recedes in her rusted-out Dart. This car feels more like home to me than the house that was my home, she thinks, heading for the expressway. Maybe someday I will meet someone who will make me not care what kind of house I live in. She adjusts her rearview mirror and instead of seeing her forehead sees the black patent brim of a cadet's summer hat. She swings the car around. Back in Charlie and Jen's driveway, she honks. She waits for the door to open, but instead the bedroom window shade flies up. Charlie leans out. His shirt is off.

"What's the matter, Dools?" He looks glad to see her.

"My hat's off to you!" she hollers, waving the hat.

Charlie turns from the window. In a moment he is back. "Jen says leave it in the driveway." He pulls the shade down.

Dooley takes the hat off. Gold-stamped letters. *Ens. Wayne Furillo.* Where are you now, Wayne? Did you make captain? Admiral? Did you chuck it all and go into computer programming? Are your legs long with the kind of hair that catches light? Are you happier now that you know how miserable you might have been? Why didn't you hang onto your hat, Wayne? Wayne Wayne wherever you are, do you like yourself better these days? Or do you want to be different and just don't know how. Well, I wish you wouldn't think

52

THE HIGH-BOUNCING LOVER

like that, Wayne. And if you have to think like that, I
wish you wouldn't say it. What's the truth anyway,
Wayne? How do you know until you make it up?

"YAHOO!" Dooley shouts and throws the hat up
in the air where it hangs against blue sky longer than
you would think possible.

THE AIR OF
MY YOUTH

Who wants their tee-eeth?" Ma says, taking an envelope out of her apron.

Ma is going to start out completely new in Florida. Her idea is to get on a plane with no luggage, only her pocketbook and cosmetic case, and move into a completely new house. There she will furnish from scratch, down to the teaspoons. She is not even taking her crystal. The past two times I've come to visit, she hasn't worn her wedding ring.

.

"Last chance for tee-eeth!" Ma waves the envelope in the air. My sister Sukey and I are sitting at the breakfast room table. We've come back home today to help. It's the last meal the four of us will ever have around this table. To celebrate, Dad's serving his beans. We talk about taking Dad's beans national. He makes the best beans in the world. You don't even know you're eating beans when you eat Dad's. They don't taste like any beans you know. He makes five varieties—

55

ALL IT TAKES

Cecil's Beans Plain, Cecil's Beans With Chicken, Cecil's Beans With Sausage, Cecil's Beans With Beef, and Cecil's Beans With Beans. This country has never known truly great beans, and my sister and I think it's ready. Cecil's Beans are complex. They're beans with overtones. They're beans al dente; you have to chew them a long time. Sukey and I think this country is ready to rethink beans. We've already figured out the label, brown butcher paper printed with gold. That echoes the concept: Humble meets dazzle.

■

"I'm not dragging these teeth with me," Ma says. She shakes the battered envelope up and down. It's the kind wedding invitations come in. She tears off a corner, tips it. Crumbs of baby teeth tumble to the table.

"Whose are they?" Sukey asks.

"You girls decide."

Dad picks out a molar with three fillings in it.

"This one looks like it's been *shot*," he says. "Whose is this?"

"Mine!" Sukey and I say at the same time.

Then we all start picking through the teeth. We pass the interesting ones around. They don't look like teeth anymore. Most of them are cracked and broken. Shards, really. You can split them with your fingernail. The roots are shriveled. Some need brushing. More than anything they resemble unpopped corn. One tooth stands out. It is tiny, white, and so perfect it could be set in a child's ring.

"Isn't this Dukie's?" I ask Ma.

She rolls her eyes. "Why would I save a dog's tooth?"

"How come you mixed our teeth together, Ma?" my sister Sukey wants to know. "How are we supposed to know whose whose?"

"The tooth fairy mixed them up, didn't she, Ma," I say.

"Fine with me, girls." Ma starts to scoop them up. "If you don't want your teeth, I'll dispose of them."

"Let's bury them!" I say to Sukey.

"Yeah!" Sukey says. "Let's bury them where we buried Dukie!"

"No," I change my mind. "Let's wait till this summer and throw them in Schroon Lake. I'm going to have my ashes scattered in Schroon Lake and I'd like to keep everything together."

I sip my coffee and think of all the good times I've had at Schroon Lake.

"You could bury them here," Ma says. "This is the house you grew up in."

"But part of me is already in the lake, Ma. I've gone swimming in that lake every summer of my life."

"Part of you is here too. You used the bathtub in this house. We have a septic tank."

So Ma is jealous of Schroon Lake. She thinks I had a better time up there than here at the soon-to-be ex-family home.

"Ma," I explain. "Swimming is different than going down the drain."

■

57

We begin to clear the table. We stack the paper cups and plates. Ma's sold the dishes already. And except for milk, she's stopped buying food. She and Dad are planning to live on whatever's left in the house until moving day. They're going to finish off the freezer, fridge, and cabinets. Just eat what's left in them even if they get beriberi doing it. The morning we come to take them to the airport, Sukey and I will probably find Ma and Dad sitting on the floor eating pimento-stuffed olives, Ritz Crackers, and hoisin sauce for breakfast.

Ma stays busy finding more things to use up, throw out, and sell. She wants to go to her new house clean. It's her last house, she says, and she wants it to have nothing from the past. It's a builder's model in Rat's Mouth, Florida, a.k.a. Boca Raton. It's got thirty-foot-high ceilings, bathrooms bigger than living rooms, and closets the size of apartments. It's got bidets and an intercom. They say they're moving because they don't like the cold. But they hate the sun. They're always being treated for skin cancer. Still, they hate the cold more. Which means they must hate the cold more than they hate skin cancer.

The mournful thing is, I'm not getting anything I want from the house I grew up in. Neither is my sister Sukey. Ma's selling it all. The dealers have already been by. They've skimmed the cream. Today we helped Ma get ready for the "A" tag sale. After that there's the "B" tag sale. Then the PennySaver. Then the Salvation Army. Ma wants to start fresh. She wants to sell it all.

"Ma! The monogrammed place plates?"

"Yes."

"The Capa di Monte lamp?"

"Yes."

"The Syrie Maugham sofa? The bronze pheasant?"

"When you really want a bronze pheasant, you can buy your own."

"But I'll buy *ours*, Ma! I'll get a better price!"

"No."

"But that's the family bronze pheasant! That was Nana's bronze pheasant!"

"I could never take money from my children," she says, pressing a self-adhesive white tag onto the bird's neck.

So we are losing everything except our baby teeth.

"Ma! No! Not Granny's Lalique vase!"

She sticks a white square on the lip.

▪

In the garage we find shovels and a flashlight. It's cold but we skip the coats.

"I'm coming, Dad," my sister Sukey says as we head toward Dukie's grave. "I'm coming the day of the tag sale and I'm buying everything I want."

"The people who run the tag sale say No family."

"Dad," Sukey says. "They're working for *you*."

"Family gets too emotional. It disrupts the sale. It makes people pay less." He's walking with his head down.

"I'm coming too," I tell Dad. "I'll wear a wig and dark glasses. I'll stuff my clothes. You'll never know it's me. But I'll be there."

We make our way across the lawn to the tree line

in back of the house. The people who bought the house will be tearing it down. They don't like the house. They bought it for the land. Hopefully they'll build the new house where the old house was, not back here by the trees. Dad shines the light on the dogwood we planted over Dukie's grave. Dukie's leather collar with the license on it still hangs there. It droops as if his old nose is still sniffing the ground. The dirt is soft. Dad starts the hole. Then my sister who is older and always goes first goes. Then me.

When the hole seems right, my sister Sukey and I take turns with the envelope and sprinkle teeth in. Dad plays the light on them. Against the dark brown earth they sparkle and look new again. They get a second wind. They look like . . . what? I know. They look like Cecil's Beans With Garlic.

We stare at the teeth some more, then cover them in reverse order. Me, then Sukey, then Dad. We watch while he stamps on the ground. I sniffle even though I haven't thought about these teeth once since they fell out.

"Ashes to ashes. Teeth to teeth," my sister Sukey says.

Then slowly we head for the house from the back lawn for the last time and I think: Someday archaeologists will discover human baby teeth over dog bones and make up whole stories about us.

■

Dad pauses at the garage door. "What are you doing?"

THE AIR OF MY YOUTH

I tell him I'll be in in a minute.

There's something strange about the night. I can't put my finger on it. I can't quite tell what it is. But even though it's strange, it's familiar. And the reason it's strange is because it's familiar even though I can't place it.

I stand out there in the starless, moonless night, a night so dark I could be blind, and try to figure it out. I stand out there in the middle of the lawn not seeing anything. I spread my arms and throw my head back. I take a deep breath through my nose. I breathe so hard my lungs shake. I breathe until they're ready to pop, and . . . that's it. I breathe again. Yes, that's definitely it. It's the air. I breathe again. Yes, that's it! It's the air of my youth. Air from twenty years ago, right after the last leaves were raked into piles and before the first snow. It smells like the night Ivan Plotnick threw gravel at my window till I slipped a parka over my nightgown and met him behind the yew bushes. It's air with pine in it and a dog not too far away.

■

I breathe till I can't smell it anymore. Smells disappear two ways. One, you get so used to them you stop noticing them. And two, there's no way to save them. The only thing that makes you remember a smell is smelling it. You don't even realize it's gone, you don't even miss it, until by chance you smell it back again.

S EAMS

I had seen Paul without him seeing me at an out-of-the-way Pottery Barn comparison shopping wineglasses with a girl in a ratty fur coat. Why was he comparison shopping wineglasses with a girl in a ratty fur coat when Betsy, sitting opposite me, was planning the wedding?

"When Paul gets back from Arizona, I'm going to ask him if he wants to get married at Ronnie and Harold's," Betsy said. "They live in New Jersey, but the house is a Stanford White with this incredible staircase. Wouldn't it be wonderful to play a daisy bouquet off a Stanford White staircase?"

I nodded. I knew Paul hadn't proposed. I knew he wasn't in Arizona. In fact, I knew he was comparison shopping wineglasses with a girl in New York. But Betsy wanted to believe that if you lived together long enough, marriage was the next step. As if relationships matured like things that inevitably mature. Stilton cheese, for example.

"Now, where exactly is he in Arizona," I asked.

"Kayenta. 'Cuando *Kayenta* el sol . . .' " she sang.

Since it seemed like it was Paul's job to tell her, not mine, I said, "Isn't that where the Navajo reservation is?"

"Well, he hasn't said too much about it. He's only been able to call once. The weather has been so perfect, they've been shooting ten-hour days."

I looked at Betsy to see if there was a flicker of anything, but her eyes were down. She looked pretty in her news anchorwoman look. She had gone from wearing Belle France dresses to preppy suits with starched white shirts to this new look: heavy silk blouses under round-shouldered jackets. I liked it. It was what a mother would have called "smart."

"I'm loving your new look," I told her.

"It's the only way to get ahead." She smiled. "So what are you doing to promote yourself these days? How are things at Jerk?"

My recent desire to be a partner at Jarvis, Enslow, Rolfe and Quinn, a midsize law firm, made this standard joke between us less appealing. I answered Betsy seriously.

"I'm trying for camaraderie," I said. "When they ask me for a drink now, I go. Also, I'm selling myself. Bragging. You know, like they do."

"It's so transparent," Betsy said. "Don't they see it?"

"And what are you doing to be taken seriously," I asked.

"I'm upgrading my blouses."

SEAMS

■

We'd met at an Executive Women's Group four years ago. It was the first meeting for both of us, held in a giant conference room on the highest floor of a utilities company on Madison Avenue. No windows. Two identically asymmetrical floral arrangements. Carpeting on the floor, walls, and ceiling. The conference table was a miracle from a primeval forest. Burled wood, sixty feet long, with no apparent seams. The room was smoky and chatty and full of women in white silk blouses with bow ties, lean, straight-haired women, ardent networkers, and as soon as I got there, I was sorry. The head of the woman who invited me rose above the other heads and nodded. I saw her weaving and bobbing in my direction. Once she reached me, I'd be trapped. But how to get out? I was too old to ever be stuck in a situation again. Too old to voluntarily be where people had to reach into their back pockets for something to say. I was too old for conference rooms filled with overeager women wondering what I could do for them. Someone coughed. I looked toward the cougher and saw her heading for the door. I began to cough too. I coughed following the cougher. Women retracted their drinks and cigarettes, making a path for us. Once outside, the cougher introduced herself.

"Betsy Motro," she said. "That kind of thing shortens your life."

■

_____

ALL IT TAKES

We began meeting regularly for lunch. There were no undercurrents to our friendship. It was easy, all out there. Wednesday lunch, a little island in the middle of the week. Two chef's salads and four cups of coffee at the same restaurant with the same waitress named Mary, a survivor of Schrafft's who retained her hair net and crisp white apron.

"The usual, ladies?" Mary always said, writing it down before we'd nod. We liked Mary. She called us ladies in a nonpolitical way. Usually, if someone called you a lady it meant you were a hetero that didn't work. If someone called you a girl, it meant you were gay. And if someone called you a woman, you were a working hetero. But here we were ladies without implication. Ladies in a small restaurant populated almost entirely by other ladies who ate alone at tables for two without removing their hats. Ladies who stared straight ahead and chewed rhythmically as if they were counting before they swallowed. Here in this restaurant every Wednesday Betsy and I were ladies, nothing more, nothing less. Here we felt free to discuss lady stuff:

"I'm going to tell you something and I want you to burn it into your brain," Betsy might say.

I'd put down my fork. "What is it?"

"Are you ready?"

"Uh-huh."

"Are you *sure* you're ready?"

"*What?*"

"*Veal chop*. Lean. High protein. Only needs broiling."

SEAMS

"The bottom line?"

"Four ounces, two hundred and ten calories."

It was here, in this little dark restaurant with its menu skewed for denture wearers, precardiacs, and postoperative fixed-income diners, that we felt free to discuss our Cuisinarts:

"What do you do when a ball of cheese gets caught between the plastic top and the grating blade?"

And our weight:

"Running around the reservoir entitles you to two bites of pizza."

And our men:

"Paul doesn't have to *say* he's going to marry me. I know by *nuance*."

It was here once a week that we could trust each other and not worry about whether revealing ourselves could hurt us. A business trip or illness was the only reason we ever canceled.

I looked forward to the Wednesday lunch every week. It felt like we were in a time lapse situation. We were like the petri dish the scientist comes back to to see what's developing. But whatever it was could not exist outside the dish. An experiment to stretch the boundaries of the friendship failed. When Betsy moved in with Paul, I had them over for dinner. It was not a successful evening. Larry didn't give Paul a chance to talk. Betsy and I watched Paul slide down his chair onto the floor. He went to sleep under the dining room table, his head resting on my foot. It was the first time I'd ever had my toes in a man's hair. The dinner continued, Larry still talking. I pretended not to think anything was strange about a thick-shouldered man snoring on my foot with his palms pressed prayerlike between his thighs. A couple of months passed, then Betsy had us over. I warned Larry not to monopolize the conversation, so he sat flexing his lips throughout dinner, drinking too much and working up to something odd. Paul, who did all the cooking, served a black meat I couldn't identify. Lyrical hunks on a white nouvelle platter. They looked like Noguchi sculptures. Betsy, stricken, announced they were turkey "parts." Stony, full of charcoal, the best one could do was gnaw at them. Paul, to his credit, finished everybody's leftovers and belched loudly. I found him refreshing. After dinner he played the tin whistle and showed us twelve years of drawings he'd made of boats seen from his living room window overlooking the Hudson. I had trouble distinguishing one from the other. When I passed them to Larry, he put his drink down on them, like a coaster, making a wet target on the *Cristoforo Columbo*. This perked Larry up immediately and he began to talk. Paul disappeared. Later, on my way to the bathroom, I caught a glimpse of him curled up on his bed, palms between his thighs.

"Wednesday?" Betsy said at the door.

"Wednesday," I said, kissing her cheek.

■

"So how was Paul's trip," I asked Betsy, flattening a butter curl against a piece of melba toast.

"He didn't want to talk about it. They're not going

to use the film. Big waste of time. You didn't mention my coat."

"It's gorgeous," I said. The mink was so dense, you couldn't tell where the pieces were sewn together.

"I paid for it myself. A gift from me to me. Tell me." She leaned closer. "Do you think it's a bad thing or a good thing that women are paying for their own fur coats?"

"I think it's good that we can afford them. But bad that we have to pay for them."

Betsy smiled, then winced. She pressed the pink table napkin to her lower lip, stared at it, then dipped the corner into her ice water.

"I forgot my lip," she said with the working part of her mouth.

I waited.

"Paul did it. I asked him to hit me and he did. I told him I had something important to announce and the only way he could stop me was to hit me. So he hit me and I stopped."

"Once I hit Larry," I told her. "But he hit me back. It's like the time I told him to leave and he said, '*You* leave. I like it here.' "

"I didn't think Paul would hit me. I mean, I didn't think he would. But then he did. Still, I didn't think he'd hurt me. But then I got into the shower —I do my crying in the shower—and I'm in there, scrubbing myself, crying nicely, when suddenly I see these red dots splash between my breasts. I couldn't imagine what they were. I thought something was leaking from upstairs or something. Where were they coming from? Red dots breaking up into tiny streams, fading into pink, then gone? They were, of course, from my lip."

"Of course," I said.

"I'll tell you what the trouble is. Paul is spending too much time on location. It's starving our relationship."

"Look, Betsy. You know the average married couple, Larry and me? We don't talk ten minutes a night. I talk more to the lady at the coffee wagon than I talk to Larry. Larry and I, we're like bumper cars. We careen into each other, then bounce off. Even on weekends. That's what it's like now. That's the way it's supposed to be."

"Not necessarily."

"Oh, really? You know why brides cry walking down the aisle? They cry because they know the good part is over. They know the courtship is finito. And they know their husbands know. They cry because they know love is strongest when you're scared of losing it."

Betsy tried to smile with her upper lip.

"I want you to be my matron of honor," she said.

■

I recognized the ratty fur coat before I saw Paul. Were these handed down in families, daughter to daughter to daughter? Were they picked up at thrift shops? It was hard to imagine someone giving it to someone as a gift. On the other hand, it was hard to imagine someone buying it, no matter how cheap it was. It wasn't the kind of coat I could imagine singing to anyone with its bald patches, droopy lining, and burst seams. It looked like it had exploded off the animals it came from. But it did stand out that night on line at the movie theater. It pulsated while Larry and I waited five couples behind it. Paul must have felt my eyes because he turned around, and although I looked down fast enough for him not to see me see him, I'm sure he saw me. Wasn't he supposed to be in Clearwater? I turned to Larry.

"I'm sick of waiting in line to see a movie. Let's go home. No movie is worth this. It's degrading."

"I told you we should get a VCR," he said. "If we had a VCR we'd never have to wait in line."

I knew I was opening myself up to the VCR argument. I was afraid if we got a VCR we'd never leave the house on weekends. Also Larry has this impulse to point things out. "Rear projection!" he shouts at the television. Or "This was Preston Sturges's swan song!" Or "Alan Ladd had to stand on a crate to kiss her!" His insider's information, gleaned from the weekly magazine he directs media for, is welcome, but not when he gives it during the film. If we got a VCR, there would be no stopping him.

"We can watch 'Saturday Night Live,' " I tell him.

"It's a rerun."

"We'll think of something."

■

"I want to look like a bride. What do you think of an antique dress? Eleanor Roosevelt kind of thing. Flat stomach, lots of lace, transparent sleeves." Betsy looked stunning in a black raglan jacket and a celadon silk blouse.

"I love it. It's just right for you."

"I'm getting tired of waiting for Paul to finalize things," Betsy said. "He's wearing me out."

"Why don't you get invitations printed up and mail them?"

Betsy brightened.

"I had a great-aunt who did that," I said. "My uncle kept her for eleven years. Then he wouldn't marry her because she wasn't a virgin. She sent out invitations."

"And?"

"And he married her."

"And?"

"And he stopped seeing her. They lived in separate apartments. She said she'd throw acid in his face if he divorced her."

"Sorry I asked," Betsy said. She appeared to be raking her chef's salad. I yearned to tell her about Paul, but I knew it would be a case of not hating the news but hating the person who gives you the news.

■

"Meet me for a drink." It was Paul, calling me at work. "I need to talk to you about Betsy."

"You can't tell me on the phone?"

"Six-thirty. You know Gin-Ray's?"

The night had just enough bite to be bracing. I got to the restaurant first and sat at the bar. I ate a whole bowl of slippery brown things, Japan's answer to the peanut, before Paul stormed in. He was out of breath, his hands shoved deep in his pockets, trench coat flapping.

"I'm reporting each and every one of these cocksuckers," he said, waving a shred of paper at my face. "Do you have any idea how many cabdrivers won't pick a guy up in a wheelchair? This poor guy in a wheelchair on Madison Avenue and nobody fucking stops! Look at this!" He stuck the paper so close to my eyes I almost leaned off the barstool. "The guy was in a *wheelchair*! You know what I'm saying?"

"Check your coat, sir?" The maître d's hands looked like wax miniatures on Paul's shoulders. Ten identical sashimis like the ones in the window. Paul spun on his stool.

"Look, Jack," he said. "I'm a big boy. If I want to check my coat, I'll check my coat. Do I look like I need help?" The man smiled and bowed. Paul turned to the bar. "A glass of club soda," he told the bartender. "And not Perrier." He ignored my drink. He did not apologize for being late. For the first time I could see what Betsy liked about him.

"You know, Paul," I said, "I don't usually meet my friends' current life partners for drinks—"

"Cut the crap," he said. "You know I'm seeing someone else. What's with this wedding shit?"

"What wedding shit," I said.

"She's planning a wedding. I've asked her to move out. I've told her I'm never going to marry her. Still every day she brings home catering menus and tablecloth swatches. I want you to tell her. Tell her I'm not marrying her."

"*You* tell her."

"I fucking told her."

"I don't want to be here," I said, standing up.

"Sit down. You know I'm seeing someone else. You've seen me with Darlene. Why don't you want to help your friend?"

Darlene. He was living with Betsy and dating a Mouseketeer. "Look," I said. "This isn't my business."

"Oh, yeah?" he said and grabbed my wrist so wonderfully I wanted to preserve the moment. I twisted my arm, pretty sure he'd grab harder. He grabbed harder, so I took what was left of his club soda and poured it in his lap. He released my wrist and I liked myself better than I liked him. On the way home I thought of his crotch freezing as he fought the winds of Riverside Drive to get to the apartment he shared with my friend Betsy.

Wednesday she looked dry as a rind. "Paul asked me to move out," Betsy said. We ordered drinks.

"Tell *him* to move out," I offered. "Look at Larry and me. I tell him to move out all the time and we're still together." Her lip, thoroughly healed, trembled. I grabbed her hand. "He's not worth it."

"Yes he is."

"At this time next year you won't even be thinking about him."

"He'd never move out. It was his apartment first. I moved in. The lease is in his name. He got his brother into that building. And his aunt and uncle and two cousins. It's practically the Paul Wein Building. His family's entrenched in that building. They're like roaches in the wall."

"It's not such a hot building, you know. You should never live in a place where you have to take two buses to get to work."

"But I like the building," Betsy said. "They keep repointing the bricks. Every time there's a bad storm, water leaks into a corner of the master bedroom and they repoint the bricks again. Once I could see right out of the building wall, right from our bed, a chink of air. I love that building. Do you think Paul means it?"

What could I say? "What do you think," I said.

"I don't think he does." Betsy smiled.

■

"I'm not meeting you anymore. Stop calling me," I told Paul when he asked me to meet him on the northeast corner of Eighty-ninth and Amsterdam. "Anything you have to say you can say over the phone."

"Be there seven-thirty Wednesday and wear jogging clothes. Your friend's happiness depends on it."

■

I waited on the corner, holding my face up, trying to find some sun to warm me. Again he was late. I heard horses behind me and figured it was riders heading for the park. Then the horses stopped so close I could smell them. I opened my eyes and looked up. Paul was looking down at me. Steam was coming out of his mouth the same as it was pouring from the horse's nostrils. He looked like a horse, the way his hair flopped over his forehead between his ears like a mane. He handed me a set of reins.

"Get on," he said.

"I haven't been on a horse since . . ." but before I could finish my sentence, Paul was off. I lowered the left stirrup and mounted. The horse kept straining toward Broadway. I had a hard time convincing him I would not consider going back to the stable. He refused to respond to a light pulling of the reins and prodding in the flanks. Maybe my jogging shoes were too soft. Maybe he knew I was in over my head. What finally did get him going was the sound cowboys make by sucking their tongues against the inside of their molars. Two of these and a "giddyap" and my horse lurched into a trot. Paul was nowhere.

I've never been a very good rider. I've always liked the feeling of being at one with the beast too much to concentrate on doing it right: heels down, toes in, back straight, wrists parallel. I can never remember to tell myself these things once the horse and I are getting along all right. I get swept up in the feeling of all those muscles working for me, pumping beneath me, all controlled by a thin slit of metal in the mouth. So I get carried away and forget what I'm supposed to do. But it is precisely when I am out of control that it is best. It is a moment beyond time, almost beyond consciousness, nothing secular about it. I was rocking along into this, heading for it, cantering lightly through a tunnel on the bridle path, when I heard the echo of a horse behind me. I slowed down and turned around.

SEAMS

Paul was flying toward me. The wind had blown his hair back, revealing a widow's peak. He was standing in his stirrups, coming at me fast. As he passed me, he raised his hand and beat the rump of my horse with his crop. It sounded like a book being slammed shut. My horse took off, passing his. I lost my stirrups, the left one first, thinking I better get this back on, then the right. But I couldn't concentrate. Joggers screamed and scattered. My horse's neck was pumping like a piston. I was hanging on by sheer knee power, pulling at the reins, wondering what sound was the opposite of a tongue sucking against the inside of a cowboy's molars when Paul rode up laughing. He grabbed my reins and I bounced to a stop.

"Why did you do that," I asked, slipping my stirrups back on.

He waited till I was settled then handed me the reins. In doing so, he brushed my breasts with his forearm. I would like to say that it was an accident. But he brushed them up handing me the reins. Then he brushed them down before taking his hand away. He did this looking at me with eyes the color of the inside of black olives. Both of us were out of breath. Although I had three layers of clothing on I felt his forearm as keenly as if he was in me. I couldn't swallow, which seemed essential before speaking.

"Now tell your girl friend it's *over*. Tell her that, *will you?*" He was trying to keep his horse from taking off, bringing it up. "Tell her that. Tell her that and *make her understand.*" Then he was gone.

"Tell her yourself, asshole!" I shouted. But the asshole part was lost and I doubt he heard any of it.

■

"There are no affordable rentals in New York," Betsy said. She'd been looking for two months. I marveled at how she was able to eat without destroying her two-tone lipstick, dark line around the outside, clear red within. "It's very strange," she continued. "He never comes home. And when he does, it's late and he slips into bed. He just slips in without saying anything. I can feel his warmth even though he never touches me. Except once. Once he did it in his sleep. I swear. He did it in his sleep. I asked him if he loved me, thinking as long as he's sleeping I'll get an honest answer, but he just said, 'Baby.' 'Baby.' Do you believe that? Do you believe they can do it in their sleep?"

"You bet," I said, recalling some of Larry's more automatic moments. "They're capable of anything."

■

"Meet Darlene," Paul said, introducing us to the girl in the ratty fur coat. Larry and I were having brunch in Soho.

"Hi," Darlene said, thrusting her hand. She wore no make-up and looked ready to like us. I found myself ready to like her back. She was a radiant kind of girl, the kind all different kinds of people are attracted to because she makes life look good. "The French toast here releases endorphins," Darlene smiled. I was glad they were on their way out or Larry would have asked them to join us.

"Isn't that the guy who lives with what's her name?" Larry asked.

"No," I said. "Try my gravlox."

•

"He's thrown himself into his work. I think this whole thing is a manifestation of a work problem. Don't you think?"

Someone had put corn in the chef's salad by mistake. We were plucking out kernels like monkeys picking nits.

"My friend Helen from work says a two-bedroom is opening up in her building," I said.

Betsy stared at me.

"It's in her line," I continued. "It overlooks the river. She thinks it's under two a month."

Betsy looked down. Her voice was tiny. "When can I see it?"

"Here's the number," I said, feeling terrible.

•

Moving day, Larry and I went over to help. Paul was there, directing things and wrapping Betsy's balloon glasses in newspaper which she would then rewrap in front of him. Still, things went smoothly till they got to the lamps. They were Paul's lamps, but Betsy had taken a night course in refinishing. She'd spent hours sanding the porcelain and spraying them pewter. "I put hours into those lamps," she told Paul.

"Aren't those the lamps Mom gave Joan when she got married?" Paul's brother Richie said. He spoke excitedly as if he could talk the lamps into his apartment. Paul studied the lamps. "Nah," he said. "I don't think these are those." He put them in the U-Haul. "Take them," he said to Betsy. "A house present."

Betsy lifted one in each hand. She held them raised in the air like trophies, then dropped them on the pavement. One broke, the other didn't.

"I never liked those lamps," she said.

Richie picked up the good one. "Well, if nobody wants it." He turned toward the building. Paul ran after him and grabbed the lamp. He handed it back to Betsy.

"Come on," he said. "You worked hard on it."

Betsy took the lamp and gave it to Richie. Paul's aunt came down with her schnauzer. "Say hi to everybody, Schnappsie," she said.

Betsy whispered to me, "I will never, ever, have to see that woman walk that dog in her bedroom slippers again. Never." Then the cousins came downstairs, and the move took on the feel of a building party. It felt like someone was about to break out jug wine and Doritos.

.

The last things on the truck were the postmodern bookcases Betsy had made for the apartment. She'd paid a carpenter to build them right in the living room.

They covered an entire wall. Wall-to-wall floor-to-ceiling white bookcases segmented into perfect squares like the grille of an English touring car. Larry helped Paul saw them in two so they could fit on the elevator. Everyone was silent while Paul and Larry struggled beneath the sliced bookcases. Richie apologized for his bad back and held the door. We watched Paul and Larry jockey the bookcases out, and I wondered if they would ever look right in the new place. I wondered if they would ever fit together again, perfectly, seamlessly. Already paint was chipping off the edges, flecks of it lying in the gutter like dot lights. Imagining Betsy trying to make them fit in the new apartment filled me with grief. I stopped wrapping the balloon glasses and even though my hands were smeared with newspaper ink, hugged her.

When the bookcases were on the U-Haul, we went upstairs to make sure nothing was left. Richie was already screwing Paul's old Chinese vegetable boxes back into the wall. The apartment didn't look like anything was missing. Betsy noticed it too.

"It's like Cheez Whiz," she said. "You take some out of the jar and half an hour later, the hole is all filled in."

∎

Betsy kept postponing lunch. She had to shop, she had to be home when the carpet man came, she had to talk to the painters. When we finally got together, she told me Darlene had moved in with Paul.

"The bed wasn't even cold," I told her.

"You went riding with him. You met him for drinks."

"What?" I said.

"You knew he was seeing somebody else. Why didn't you tell me?"

There was only one way she could have known.

"Why did you do that?" Betsy shook her head from side to side. "Why?"

Well, I thought. I am recognizing a moment here. A point of no return. My relationship with Betsy will never be the same from this moment. Things will be forever altered. It's like overhearing your mother speak badly about your father. Or discovering a teacher you've loved grades papers without reading them. It's like seeing a partner in your law firm who specializes in morality cases wheel out of a gay bar with a runaway on his arm. Or passing a garbage can filled with empty cans of institutional marinara sauce outside your favorite home-style Italian restaurant. The guard is up. The trust is down. Something is dead. It's not bitterness or an inability to forgive. It's an evolution brought on by a piece of knowledge. A small tear or opening. An enlightenment that defines a relationship in a new way. A way from which there is no going back.

"Well," Betsy was waiting, genuinely interested. "I really want to know. Why did you do that? Why did you see him? Why didn't you tell me?"

"He said it was in your interest. He was very insistent. I tried to say no to him. I did say no. He just kept on insisting. In fact, he was a raving lunatic. And he never said anything that I believed or that could be helpful."

"Still," Betsy said. "You could have told me. You *should* have told me."

"The whole thing made me sick. Please believe me. He would call, insisting it was in your interest, then say nothing in your interest."

"Well, what did he say that *wasn't* in my interest?" Betsy leaned across the table.

"Mainly that I should tell you it was over."

"Oh." Betsy pulled back. "I see. But of course you didn't pass that on."

"Of course," I said, then realized she was being sarcastic. "Betsy. Please. It wasn't my business. You would have despised me."

"You didn't have to go, you know. Especially the second time."

I was quiet for a moment, thinking this over. "Betsy," I said. "Why do you think Paul told you we met?"

"He told me when I asked him."

"You asked him if we met?" I put my fork down.

"You've been interested in him since that first night. It was obvious from the minute he fell asleep under your table."

"Well," I said. "That's news to me."

"In fact, it occurred to me that night that he might be seeing *you* on the side all along."

I thought of signaling Mary then. I thought of asking for the check. But I was fascinated. And even though it was getting unpleasant, I wanted to see the thing through. Wednesday lunch. I could feel it slipping through my fingers.

"So tell me, Betsy. Do you hate me?"

"Some things can never be understood," she said.

■

The next time we met it was at a new place. The old place was being razed as part of a block assemblage and we had Cobb salad because they didn't have chef's salad. I kept wondering if it hadn't been for me finding the new apartment, would Betsy still be living with Paul? I wondered, too, when she would stop hating me for knowing something I never wanted to know. It's terrible knowing something you don't want to know, something someone is anxious to put behind them. Every time they see you, they see the thing they want to forget. Once Betsy invited me up to the new apartment for lunch. She'd done wonderful things with it. Green marble floor tiles in the kitchen. Forty-inch-square knife-edge pillows. Bigger-than-life accessories. All the things Paul didn't like. It's a compromise in terms of light. But the apartment is prewar and only one bus line from work. And it reflects one person's point of view, one person's taste, seamless except for the place the bookcases meet. There you see a shadow. But it is a shadow you see only if you know that once those bookcases were cut in half and then, at a later date, put back together again.

WHICH IS BETTER?

Bobby kicks Kate in an Oriental way, swift and jabbing under the rib cage. He puts his whole body into it. Del watches from the upstairs bathroom window. Bobby gives it all he's got. He's going to kill her, Del thinks. He's going to kill her and get sent to a youth correctional facility. He'll get sodomized there by someone in Administration and wind up on drugs. He'll blame it all on me then creep into my bedroom late at night and shoot me at close range with a gun made from sink parts.

Bobby follows through with a bash on the head. Kate screams and runs toward the house.

I saw that! Del considers shouting from the upstairs bathroom window. Then she asks herself, Which is better? If I don't interfere, Bobby will have to make peace with Kate on his own, before she can tell on him and get him into trouble. If I do interfere, I will have to hear each side of the story, how each one is justified. I will also blow Bobby's cover. It's not that he thinks he is always good. It's that it's important to him to think that *I* think he is always good.

ALL IT TAKES

So Del watches and does nothing. On this unseasonably warm fall day, when only an adult would be foolish enough to wear fall clothes, Del watches the scenario unfold from the upstairs bathroom window. For a moment the frame is empty. Then Kate sails in on Bobby's new dirt bike. He has paid dearly for the joy of kicking her.

•

Del watches Kate tool around the lawn. She leans into it, going so fast she keeps losing the pedals. Then Kate makes the mistake of laughing so Bobby runs after her. He gets a grip on the back of Kate's T-shirt and makes her dismount. Then he wipes the pedals clean with the hem of Kate's skirt. Bobby likes clean pedals. He shines both sides of his shoes. Spying on her children, Del feels guilty. Not because she is doing something sneaky, but because she knows how differently the children would behave if they knew she was watching.

Del turns from the window and starts wiping around the sink. In the apartment, a cleaning lady comes once a week. But here in the country it's Del's job. Reaching for the Comet, she wonders if cave women cleaned. She wonders who it was that said, "Housework is like stringing beads on a thread that has no knot." A pioneer woman? A Russian peasant? A Mennonite? She wonders why she hates cleaning so much, why it makes her hate her family. Every time Del picks a sock off an easy chair, or scratches at the ring inside the toilet bowl with a smelly yellow bristle brush, she threatens out

WHICH IS BETTER?

loud, GET ME OUTA HERE! GET ME OUTA HERE *NOW!* hitting a dazzling high C on the *NOW!* No one seems to have heard her yet. But then, after she has used the towels that need to be washed to wash out the sink and the tub and wipe the floor, she hits her trance rhythm and no longer seems to mind the irony of a clean bathroom. A clean bathroom only goes downhill. Bobby and Kal splattering the seat, the floor, the base of the toilet in festering, hard-to-reach places. Sometimes they hit the wall. Kate's glob of virgin toothpaste on the side of the sink. Spilled cough medicine, dirty underware, stray shoes. Hair. Truly, the only one who cares about keeping a bathroom clean is the one who has to clean it.

■

Del tries not to consider the implications of this. She hates her smallness. Other women must feel pride and pleasure in the creation of a spotless bathroom. Del adds Lack of Joy in Making a Nice Home to the long list of things she finds wrong with herself. Why can't she ever feel the glow of accomplishment, the radiance of satisfaction other women get from a well-maintained home? She does get that glow when other people do it for her. She would pay to have a lady like herself come in and tease dirt out from between the toilet seat joints. Then she would enter the bathroom warmly and graciously, full of compliments.

■

Del picks a flat black bug off the bathtub rim. She hasn't had the house long enough to understand the patterns of the bugs yet. Some mornings when she enters the bathroom, there are heaps of carcasses on the sink beneath the medicine chest light. Airy drifts of insect bodies, light as dust. These she picks up with gobs of wet toilet paper, then flushes. What do other women do? Sometimes all the window sills are lined with dead flies, belly up, legs folded into themselves. They weren't there the night before. These she sweeps up with a piece of dry toilet paper, careful not to crunch them, and also flushes. Sometimes there are live black beetles, small ones, not roaches, crisscrossing the linoleum. These she never kills. There are more where they came from. And if she does not kill them she will not have to clean them up.

Still holding the flat black bug from the bathtub rim, Del looks out the window again. The children are in the upper right-hand corner, watching. Kal enters from the left on his seated mower. She notices for the first time a bald spot on the back of his head near the top. Not really bald, but thinning. She watches the kids run toward him. Del respects Kal for doing this work, even though he seems to love it, even though every other weekend, it takes half a day. She watches Kal exit the window frame and wishes she didn't feel uneasy about him acting like a farmer when he is on the mower. His voice gets twangy on the mornings he mows. What right do I have for resenting this? Del thinks. What is so bad about playacting at forty-two? Would I respect him more if he screamed, GET ME

WHICH IS BETTER?

OUTA HERE! GET ME OUTA HERE *NOW*! every time he mowed? Which is better? A husband who resents his chores? Or a wife who thinks he's strange for not minding them? Oh twisted sister, Del thinks. Twisted, twisted. She watches Kal put the mower in neutral and carry the clippings to the compost pile. She drops the flat black bug into the toilet and flushes. When the water settles, the bug is still there.

"Hi, everybody!" Del yells out the window. Kate and Bobby look up squinting. They have not learned to shield their eyes when the sun is in them. "Want some lemonade?"

■

Del beats them to the kitchen. She finds three lemons in the vegetable bin. Kate holds the kitchen door open for Bobby, and Del automatically says, "You're letting bugs in!" Why is she the only one who makes the connection between an open door and letting bugs in?

Bobby sees the lemons. "Oh," he says. "*Real* lemonade?"

"Real lemonade is better than fake lemonade," Del says.

"No it isn't," Kate says. "Real lemonade is gross."

"Oh really?" Del hopes what she is about to say will not sound like a learning experience. Anytime she tries to teach the children something they roll their eyes. Sometimes her sentences are left hanging in the air like abandoned spider webs. "What's gross about real lemonade?"

"There are things in it," Kate says.

"Pulp, Dumbo," Bobby explains.

"Ma! He called me Dumbo!"

"Are you dumb?" Del asks Kate.

"No," Kate says.

"Then what do you care what he calls you?"

"Dumbo is an elephant," Kate says.

"All right then Kate. Are you an elephant?"

Kate thinks, shakes her head.

Del cuts the lemons and adds, "You know what you tell someone who calls you a mean name? You say, 'Some people call other people what they themselves are.' That's what you say. Try it, honey."

" 'Some other people call you them?' " Kate says.

Del puts her knife down. "You know what's good? Try this. 'I can always count on you for a put-down.' "

"If I'm a Dumbo," Kate says, "he's an afterbirth."

The weekend before, Del had taken Kate and Bobby to see the cows at the dairy farm down the road. One had just delivered. A torn red bag of afterbirth hung between her legs. The children stood with their mouths open. Finally, it was Bobby who looked away. He went to the new calf and let it suck his thumb. But Kate kept staring at the smoking afterbirth. She wanted to know what her afterbirth had looked like and where it was now and what it was for and if it had feelings. And who did it belong to? Was it hers? Was it Del's? This kind of obsession happens regularly. It pleases Del because she thinks it will serve Kate well in school. While Bobby drifts from one thing to another, like a soft pastel with no edges, Kate focuses on one thing to the exclusion of everything else. The following day, Kate begged to be taken back to see the cow. The afterbirth was still there, still attached, browner, more ragged, smaller, and still bloody.

"I can't be afterbirth, Dumbo," Bobby laughs. "Afterbirth isn't alive."

"All right! Who wants real lemonade and who wants fake?"

"Fake!" Both children raise their hands. Where have I gone wrong? Del wonders. Why do they like the imitations of things better than the real things? With hamburgers, McDonald's is the criterion. When Del makes hamburgers at home, the children complain because they are not flat and gray. They complain because homemade burgers are pink inside and juicy. They prefer canned corn to corn on the cob. TV to movies. Movies to plays. Comics to books. Velcro to shoelaces.

If my fake is their real, Del wonders, what do they think of my love? Is my love real or fake? Is real love what they see on "The Cosby Show" and "Family Ties"? Or is my love real love, the love that was formed on "Father Knows Best" and "Make Room for Daddy"?

"Look what's in here." Del squints, reading the pink lemonade label. "Potassium citrate, magnesium oxide, sodium phosphate, artificial coloring, artificial flavoring, phenylalanine."

"If we could buy those things," Kate wants to know, "could we make homemade fake lemonade?"

■

It seems important to Del to prove to the children that fake lemonade is not as good as real lemonade.

"You know what," she says. "We're going to take a taste test. How about that? I'm going to make real lemonade and fake lemonade and give you a small cup of each, and then you'll tell me which is better."

"I'm gonna like pink better," Bobby says.

"Will you blindfold us?" Kate wants to know.

"And I am going to strain it to make the test fair," Del continues, "even though pulp is good for you."

"How?" Kate says.

"Roughage. And because it tells you the lemonade is real. It's like finding a piece of egg shell in your scrambled eggs. You know real eggs were used."

"What do fake eggs taste like?" Kate wants to know.

"Pink lemonade," Del says.

"I don't want to be blindfolded." Bobby's voice has that wavering quality that means he feels strongly enough about something to cry.

"How come, honey?" Del says carefully. "You don't have to. But how come?"

"Because part of the reason I like it is *because* it's pink. I like the *color*. It's not fair to blindfold me if the color's one of the reasons I like it."

He's trembling now. The boy who tried to kill his sister is aquiver. He can try to kill his sister, Del thinks, but he weeps over the hint of an injustice.

"Then you don't have to be blindfolded," Del says.

"Me neither." Kate folds her arms over her chest.

WHICH IS BETTER?

"All right. All right. Nobody has to be blind-folded. Never mind. We don't need blindfolds. It's okay. No blindfolds. Forget the blindfolds. Who needs blindfolds? What's a blindfold, anyway?" GET ME OUTA HERE! Del thinks. GET ME OUTA HERE *NOW!* Amen! Ta ta! So long! Oy vey! Bye-bye, my love! and Ciao!

▪

The three of them, Del and her two children, Bobby and Kate, sit around the kitchen table while Del pours four cups of lemonade. Del sits with the sponge to her right so as Kate and Bobby spill she can soak it up before it drips onto the floor and she has to clean that too. Simultaneously, they put their cups down and listen. They are hearing an absence of noise. They are hearing silence. Kal has turned off the mower. They had been unaware of the whirr of the mower until Kal turned it off. How odd, Del thinks, not to hear a particular sound until the moment that sounds stops.

Kal opens the screen door. He pauses with his fist on the doorjamb and surveys his family drinking lemonade together at the kitchen table as if he has just reconfirmed that he lives in a Norman Rockwell illustration. Kal sees them like this often. His eyes get moist from his good fortune. Del envies this. Why can't she see the family the way he does? Is it because he sees the family that way that they act that way with him? If she believed they were Norman Rockwell people, would they behave like Norman Rockwell people with her? Do they behave like Francis Bacon people

---

93

with her because she treats them the way she does? Where did it start? Where will it end? How will this family ever get better if he keeps seeing them as well to start with? Del decides to treat Kal like a Norman Rockwell father and see how it works. She has a plan. Something wonderful is about to happen.

■

"Sit down, honey," Del says, rising, pulling out a chair for him. In one stroke she has gotten Kal to join them and to shut the screen door without telling him to. It crosses her mind that she will die an early death from thinking so much. She'll enervate her brain. "You're about to participate in an experiment," she says.

"I could use some lemonade." Kal reaches for the cup with pink lemonade in it.

"Wait." Del covers the cup with her hand. "This is a taste test. It's real lemonade versus fake lemonade. You taste both lemonades, then put the winning cup in the center of the table. Close your eyes."

"Don't close them, Daddy!" Bobby shouts. "She can't make you!"

"It's not fair," Kate says.

"I don't care," Kal says. "Eyes open, eyes closed. It doesn't matter. I don't know what you're trying to prove, though."

"Please, Kal," Del says. "We're having fun. Please."

Bobby goes first. He sips real, pink, real, pink, pink, pink, pink and pushes his pink cup to the center of the table.

94

WHICH IS BETTER?

Then Kate. She sips pink, real, real, pink, pink, real, pink and pushes her pink cup to the center of the table.

Then Kal clenches his eyelids and feels along the table.

"Just a minute," Del says, shifting the cups around like a magician doing the shell and pea trick. She puts one cup in Kal's left hand and one in his right.

Kal takes a sip from each. He asks Del for a saltine to cleanse his palate. He sniffs the cups. Kal sips pink, real, pink, real, pink, real. He swishes each sip around in his mouth as if it is Château Margaux, 1969. He says "Ahhhhh" after he swallows. Then he sits back in his chair and thinks. The children watch him, waiting. Kal starts to slide the real cup toward the middle of the table, takes another sip of each, hesitates, then slides the pink cup over to Kate's and Bobby's. He opens his eyes. He looks around the table. The children are beaming.

"See?" Kate says. "Fake is better."

∎

In bed, Del reads the parts of the newspaper she has saved all week for when she has time to read. If she looks straight ahead, she can see the reflection of Kal in the bedroom window. He is backlit in the bathroom, standing in front of the long mirror, performing his prebed ritual. At first she was ashamed, watching him this way, without his knowing it. But now she is indifferent. He spends more time taking care of his teeth than I take taking care of all of me, she thinks.

ALL IT TAKES

She watches as he brushes, flosses then massages with special toothpicks. He uses the new tool, a pointed spiral brush on a long stick that he rotates between his teeth at the base of his gums. He does all this baring his teeth, the same face that hovers over her in bed. He spends more time on his teeth than he spends on me, Del thinks. Which is better? Being toothless but attentive? Or having great teeth and a neglected wife? If he didn't spend twenty minutes in front of the mirror every night, would those twenty minutes be mine? Do I even want them? What would I do with them?

After the teeth, he explores his face. He seeks and destroys anything that shouldn't be there. Then, before he puts his pajama top on, he rubs his chest and examines his muscles. He examines them the same way Del looks in the mirror. He knows the angles he can count on, the ones that show him what it is he wants to see. He crosses his arms in front of his chest and uses his knuckles to plump his biceps. He twists from front to side, seeing more of what he wants and less of what he doesn't. Del does this when she looks at herself in the mirror too. She can make it so there's no sag under her chin and her eyes sparkle. She has reached the stage where she has stopped seeking glimpses of herself in store windows and chance mirrors. She will no longer look at herself unprepared. With this in mind, she extends her neck and drops a shoulder so that her jawline firms and her nightgown slips down on one side.

Kal, satisfied, turns out the bathroom light and slides into bed beside Del. Their signals to each other

have become so refined that Kal knows if Del is reading when he gets into bed (instead of sleeping with her
back to him) and if she is wearing a nightgown with one
shoulder down, and if her neck looks awkward, it's
okay. Just to double-check, he shoots an exploratory
toe in her direction. She answers by turning her foot
toward his. He slides his hand up under her nightgown
until it finds a breast. He pinches her nipple and twists
it as if he is fine-tuning a radio dial. Oh! she says then
kisses his shoulder. It is faintly sticky, almost gummy
from the work he has done today. All that attention
to the teeth, and no shower. Still, it smells sexy and
tastes salty so she sucks the skin on his neck, working her way up to his ear. When she gets there, she
whispers, "Why did you say you liked the pink lemonade better?"

He moves to her other nipple, performing the
identical maneuver. This time it feels to Del as if he is
tapping out the Morse code, not that she doesn't like it,
not that she minds.

"Because I did." He moves his mouth there.

"You couldn't have," she says, pulling him off by
the hair. "Real is better than fake."

"Yeah? You like real? How's this for real? This is
real, isn't it?" He rolls on top of her, knees her legs
open and in three thrusts is all the way in. "What do
you think? Is this real enough for you?"

She doesn't answer.

"I asked you something. Is this real enough or
what?"

"Um-hm," Del says. "Yup."

ALL IT TAKES

■

Afterward, after the slow round and round that Del likes and the machine gun type thing that Kal likes, after her gnawing of his shoulder because she likes to, and the grabbing of his scrotum because he likes that, and his pulling and pressing of her buttocks like an accordion because he thinks she likes that and he likes doing it, and his squeezing together of her legs between his tight so she can feel him more even if that's not what she wants, Del thinks: There are two kinds of touching. The touch of someone who is responding to you out of passion without thinking. And the touch of someone who is doing what they think they are supposed to be doing, the touch of someone trying to please. Which is better? Del wonders and instantly knows. The second one is no good at all. It is awful to be touched out of doing the right thing, out of trying to please. Passion is the only good touch there is. Passion is real. Doing the right thing is fake.

She explains this to Kal as he is falling asleep. He rolls over and drops his hand between her legs. After a moment, she stops protesting. When he takes his hand away before she wants him to, she grabs him hard by the wrist and puts his hand back. He laughs when she asks him to please not stop until, at last, she grabs his wrist a second time with the strength that always surprises him, and pins his hand to the mattress.

■

WHICH IS BETTER?

Del puts her palm over her heart. She brings her knees up to her chest. Kal pulls the quilt over his shoulders. The room feels cold. They both notice it. It is a sudden and temporary cold, like a cloud passing in front of the sun on a warm day at the beach. It's a cold like a warning, brief and unexpected, impossible to ignore.

"How bad was that?" Kal asks, twisting away from her, taking too much cover. "How fake do you call that?"

"You took their side," Del says. "You ganged up on me."

"You make a rotten lemonade."

"What?"

"You make lemonade as if it's supposed to be good for you." Kal yawns. "You never put enough sugar in."

"No one's ever complained about my lemonade before. Everybody always loves my lemonade."

"Can we let this go till morning, Del? Can we sleep on it?"

Del slides down the bed and rests her head against the pillow. She listens to the wind beat pine tassels against the window. Which is better? she wonders. A man who loves you enough to tell you the truth? Or a man who loves you enough not to hurt you. Thinks Too Much, Del adds to her list of things she can't stand about herself. Thinks Too Much But Can't For The Life Of Her Stop.

Something wet in the dark

I cried at the airport when I said good-bye to my sister. She was leaving New York for good, moving to Florida with her one-year-old Natey who squirmed on the inorganic Day-Glo carpet of Eastern's Gate 20.

I cried from the time we hit the Triborough. I kept it up on the Grand Central, down into short-term parking, clear through the entrance doors, past security and over by the departure gate. I kept it up while she put Natey down on his belly—Natey fat, bald, and barefoot—so he could pound the Day-Glo blue carpet with his fists.

I love my sister most when she is leaving me. The rest of the time we fight. We fought all the time growing up. All the time nonstop. We fought with hairbrushes, fingernails, and spit. We fought over clothes, boys, the phone. We fought whenever we could, whenever there was nothing better to do. She was older, bigger, and stronger, but I was not afraid to die. We did things to each other with wire hangers. Once she had a finger sewn back on. The lead from a pencil

101

is still in my leg. Perhaps someday that lead will dislodge itself and circulate up to my heart. Born eighteen months apart, two girls, both accidents, born to fight.

The day she left for college, I cried all over the lobby.

Then I went to visit her for a weekend.

"You didn't bring a towel?" she screamed. "Jesus Christ!"

"I don't get a towel?" I screamed back. "What's a towel?"

"I get you a date, and now you want a towel?"

■

Six years later she married Rick and I cried all over the synagogue. I cried walking down the aisle, standing beneath the huppah, shaking hands on the reception line. I cried clear through catching the bouquet and throwing the rice. I had to be supported, physically, when Rick's Camaro made a right on 88th turning out of sight down to Park.

But all of that crying was just a warm-up for today. All of that was a dress rehearsal. Florida was leaving the state. Florida was the farthest she had ever gone. Why did she have to leave me? Why did she have to take Natey? Why did they have to go to a place you had to pretend it was winter?

"Be careful," I told her, hugging her tight. "The alligators are *above* ground there."

Natey threw up something that looked like kielbasa. It clotted without spreading.

"I can't take it," I told my sister.

She put her arm around my shoulders and squeezed.

"It's not too late to change your mind," I told her. "Anything can be undone. Fifty percent of all marriages end in divorce."

By this I meant she didn't have to go to Florida just because Rick could get tenure teaching medieval law there. She didn't have to go to a place where Don Johnson was a topic. She didn't have to take Natey where the red ants were as big as palmetto bugs and the palmetto bugs were as big as birds. She didn't have to leave me.

"Look," she said, digging into her pocketbook. "We'll be here till we find a real place."

"Tonight," I snatched the paper. "I'll call you tonight. What time do you land?"

She took out her ticket and checked her ETA. I glanced at the number she had given me. (305) 667-9066. Something hit me.

"You're not going to believe this." I blew my nose. "The last three digits of your phone number are the first three digits of my social security number."

"Is that right?" she said, checking on Natey. He had stopped squirming. He seemed to be spinning. He went around and around on his belly like a compass on the North Pole. "I guess I ought to clean that up," she said. We stared at the stuff. It looked like the fake throw-up you can buy at T-shirt and whoopee cushion stores near 42nd and Broadway. "You don't want to clean that up," my sister said. "Do you?"

I didn't answer. She took a "See Florida Like a Native" brochure out of her ticket envelope and used it. The stuff came up whole. She walked it to a garbage can.

"Well," I said, "The good news is, it's going to be easy to remember your phone number."

"Don't bother. This place is only temporary. It has a metal roof."

"Well, parts of Florida have to be nice," I tried to console her. "I mean, the Kennedys go down there. Donald Trump."

"Rick says 110th Street is a dump."

"110th Street? One hundred and ten? We grew up at 110 Riverside Drive!"

■

We watched Natey. He seemed to be trying to roll over. His stomach was so round and his width so close to his length that what he wanted to do had to violate some law of physics.

"Dr. Delgado says Natey will grow out of this," my sister said. "It's this thing with fat babies. They can't turn over. They're like turtles. All they can do is flail."

"What do you think? Should we flip him?"

"That depends what book you read," my sister said. "I can choose between leaving him alone and building his frustration tolerance. Or showing him that his mother will always be there to help him."

A lot of people started looking at Natey. Who would believe a baby could sweat like that? He began to grunt. "This isn't so unusual, you know," my sister said. "There's a name for this. Dr. Delgado says it's called Swimmer Puppy Syndrome."

"Know what?" I said to my sister. "Dr. Delgado's office is on East 38th Street and I weigh 138. I never thought of that before."

I began to cry all over again, thinking I'd never be able to help my sister take Natey to the pediatrician's again. I'd never sit in that office again with the wooden stool that had a magnifying glass in the seat and the tailless pink horse with one eye.

"Look." My sister put an arm around me. "Dr. Delgado's number is 929-7420. Can you do anything with that?"

"929. September 29. Dad's birthday."

"Try Dad's number."

"831-1396? Piece of cake. Grandpa Jake is 83. January 13 is Natey's birthday. We left P.S. 9 after the 6th grade."

"Okay," my sister said. "What about 382-1410?"

"Not familiar," I said. "Doesn't ring a bell. But here goes: You graduated college in 3 years in '82, and 82 is the last two numbers of your old home phone in reverse. The 14th is Valentine's Day, Schweetheart. And 10 stands for the Commandments. Add 10 to 14 and you get 24 or 2 and 4, which equals 6, the month of June, when Mom and Dad got married. That number is *loaded*," I said. "Whose is it?"

"I made it up."

"You did a number on me?"

"A *number* number."

"I mind that," I told her. "I mind that you got a kick out of doing that."

"Are they calling our flight?" My sister ignored me.

"But what we've done here today"—I pretended not to hear her—"what we've proven, is that we're all hooked up to each other. We're all connected. You. Me. The world. No matter where you go or who you are you're never more than a number away from anyone. That given enough information about a person, their Citicard, their Am Ex, their height, weight, shoe size, year of birth, we can find a link, a connection. We are all close." The first class passengers began to board. "We are all not far." My voice rose. "We are all *connected!*"

She scooped Natey off the floor. She had to bend her knees to pick him up. He continued to swim in her arms as if he thought he was still on the carpet. I kissed his round shoulders. I kissed his round knees. I kissed his folds. I kissed his creases. I kissed places his mother didn't know he had. I squeezed whatever was available and stuck my nose in his neck, which had short Day-Glo blue fibers on it and smelled like a cheese from some small town in Germany.

Then I kissed my sister. My sister, my half. Natey was getting squashed between us. He kicked and pushed. For a moment I had the sensation that he was in me, that this was what it feels like when you're pregnant and the baby kicks, when you put your hand on your stomach and say, "I feel life." And I thought about last night. Last night in her apartment while we put the finishing touches on the packing, my sister asked me if

I would consider giving her one of my kidneys, should she ever need it.

"You're the closest genetic donor," she said. "Besides, I'm not asking for myself. It's not just me I'm thinking about. I have Natey now. You have no one."

I didn't answer right away. It wasn't that I wouldn't do anything for her and Natey. She was right. I didn't have a husband. I didn't have a baby. I had no one else to love. My entire love capacity was being used on them. They were it. But I didn't answer right away because how could I be sure what my situation would be when she needed it? How did I know how I'd feel then? Suppose one of my kidneys was on the fritz? What if both my kidneys were superb, but later one went sour? Could I get my good one back? Would she offer? Would I have the nerve to ask?

"Well, what about me?" My voice wobbled. "If I needed a kidney, would you give me one?"

I suppose she didn't answer because the answer was no, only she couldn't come out and say no because then I could say, Well I won't give you one of mine either. I suppose both of us wanted to hang onto our kidneys as long as we could and not commit until we could really evaluate the circumstances. Were her kidneys more important than mine because she had Rick and Natey and all I had was someone who had Rick and Natey?

"INVALIDS AND PEOPLE TRAVELING WITH SMALL CHILDREN MAY BOARD NEXT!"

I rubbed in closer to them. The three of us moved

toward the gate, hugging each other like the last epi-
sode of "The Mary Tyler Moore Show." I was crying
with abandon and had lost complete control of the
corners of my mouth.

"Wait!" I said. "Don't go! Get on last! People
won't push! Last is best!"

"Thanksgiving's right around the corner. Two
months, Baby."

She separated Natey and herself from me. I felt
air where they had been.

"Look." My voice broke like Oliver North's. "If
I'm not married, if I don't have a child, if I'm not
planning to have a child, if I'm healthy and have
complete medical approval and maybe a signed consent
that if any of these things changed in any way, shape,
or form I could have it back, you can have the kidney,
any one, left or right, name it." I got louder. "It's yours
for the asking!" People turned around. "BONE MAR-
ROW! LIVER LOBES! RETINAS AND CORNEAS!
I'LL TRADE YOU TWO ISLETS OF LANGERHANS
FOR A SPLEEN!"

My sister frowned. "You don't really *need* a spleen,
Baby. They're vestigial."

She studied me for a moment then moved closer.
She was smiling. Her face was filled with love. I raised
my lips one last time. She thrust her tongue in my
mouth.

"CREEPONI!" I screamed. "SLEAZOID! HOW
COULD YOU DO THAT? WHY DID YOU DO THAT?"

She backed away, laughing, jiggling Natey. The
sensation of her tongue in my mouth was as baroque as

taking a bath in jello or petting a skunk or having your foot sink into something wet in the dark. It violated some law of nature, like bending down in an up elevator.

I watched as she disappeared into the flexible hose tunnel. There was a flash of Natey's round heel sticking out of the diaper bag before they vanished completely. God, I thought. I had no idea my sister loved me so much. She loves me enough to do anything to get me not to miss her. My sister loves me enough to try to make me love her less.

I sat down on a molded Day-Glo blue chair and wondered what I was feeling. The height of rage? The height of love? The height of grief? The height of what? Were all heights the same? Was there a difference?

I wiped my palm across my mouth and ran my tongue down my sleeve. She would miss me. He would miss me. They would miss me. Amo. Amas. Amat. The next time I saw Natey, he would probably be wearing miniature Reeboks with Velcro closings. What can you do? Some things are beyond figuring. It's like Ethel Zimmerman changing her name to Ethel Merman and then years later Bob Zimmerman changing his to Dylan.

Reckless Dreamer

Something about the shape of the man walking toward Nancy makes her eyes dart even though Jeff is taking her picture. She is leaning against the side of their snow-covered car. The children are sitting on the roof of the car. It is the first big snow of the year.

Jeff snaps the picture, smiles through his beard, and follows Nancy's eyes to the bearish man walking with his head down. The man's hands are rammed in his pockets. He is wearing the kind of clothes people who don't go out in the snow wear when they have to go out in the snow. Below his lined trench coat Nancy sees he's tucked the pants from a suit into the top of his brown socks. The seams of his cordovans flex through black rubbers. He is walking with his head down so if he slips he will be ready.

As the man closes in on the family posing by their snow-buried car, he looks up and meets the eyes of the mother, Nancy. She smiles big, knowing her cheeks are red and that she looks sculptural when her knitted hat is down over her eyebrows covering her hair and forehead. The man smiles back at Nancy, then his eyes move to Jeff. He takes Jeff in, then the children. His pace does not slow as he enters their circle.

"Hello!" Nancy says and can't think of anything else. The man nods. Then Jeff smiles at the man and the man smiles back. Nancy wonders what Jeff is thinking. He does not know the man. She does.

She knows he is living in the city again. She knows this because every year, for the past fourteen years, she has looked him up in the phone book each time the new one is delivered. For twelve years, after they stopped seeing each other, his name had been missing. Wherever she traveled, for business or pleasure, Nancy looked him up in the local phone book. Ogunquit, Maine. Lexington, Kentucky. Saranac Lake, New York. Rochester, Minnesota. Deerfield, Illinois. Key Largo, Florida. Sharon, Connecticut. Wappingers Falls. Now, for the past two years, his name has been back in the local phone book. Occasionally she calls his number, listens to his voice, and hangs up. Occasionally she receives a call from someone who listens to her voice say hello but that person doesn't say anything either. When this happens, Nancy says, "Please don't be shy. I want to talk to you too." Then the person hangs up. After she receives one of these silent phone calls, Nancy hangs up then dials the man, hoping to create a connection. Sometimes he answers. Sometimes he doesn't. She knows this is no positive indication that he is making the calls. Does everyone, she wonders, get these calls? Probably yes. But if they were innocent wrong numbers wouldn't the caller say sorry or hang up immediately? If these were innocent wrong numbers, why would the caller wait there, listening, breathing into the mouthpiece?

She watches as the man stares at Jeff in passing. Nancy tries to see Jeff through his eyes. So she married someone her own age. Academic type, beard. Look how thin his legs are. Look how easily he grins. Doesn't even know me. An indiscriminate grinner. Prosaic. Talks too loud at dinner parties. Corners people.

Nancy knows from the phone book that the man lives only four blocks away. It seems incredible that it has taken them all this time to run into each other. So many times Nancy has left the apartment thinking, Today's the day I'm going to run into him. And now it is the day and she hasn't thought about him at all this morning. And now he is seeing her, unrehearsed, sculptural, with two children and a thin-legged man who smiles easily.

Nancy follows the man's back down the street. He is probably on his way home after trying to buy milk and cheese, staples for his solitary life. He probably forgot the deli is closed on Sunday. Or maybe he was at the cash machine, saving his banking for Sunday so he'd have a reason to get dressed. Nancy follows his back and is surprised. The man does not turn toward his address. Instead he heads for the park, where they are going.

■

Jeff helps the children down from the car. They slither off the roof into his arms. Safely down, they break away. Max, the boy, hurls his body into drifts formed by the snowplow. The snow is taller than he is. Goldie, the girl, follows him.

"Watch out for the yellow snow!" Nancy screams. They ignore her, laughing, rolling in it, friends through distraction. Indoors, where there is nothing better to do, they fight all the time. Outside they never fight. Nancy looks at Jeff. He is so slender and healthy looking. *Outside we never fight either.*

The man has almost disappeared. Nancy sees him turn into the park. It seems that he is heading for the sledding hill. Yes, the sledding hill would be the only reason he would turn there. She will see him at the sledding hill if he doesn't leave. But why the sledding hill? What could he want there? Wouldn't she have heard if there were a wife and children?

"Come on, kids!" Nancy says, walking ahead of them. What if he stared at them because he didn't know who they were and wondered why they were smiling? Fourteen years is a long time not to see someone. What if he didn't remember her at all? Would it be like the man who had kissed her at the office Christmas party? The man who wouldn't let her dance with anyone else? Almost a stranger and yet he had monopolized her, insisted on dancing every dance with her. And he had kissed her. After she had gotten her coat from the checkroom, he had pushed her into a phone booth, backing her up against the wall, taking her by surprise. The next day she had taken the elevator up to his office, stormed through the door, and said, "Did that kiss mean to you what it meant to me?" He'd looked up, faintly irritated. "What kiss?" he'd said and gone back to his work.

RECKLESS DREAMER

∎

They crunch through the snow and enter the park. Jeff pulls Max and Goldie on the sled. They keep forgetting to steer. They roll off, twisted together, into shoveled snow along the path.

"Watch out for the yellow snow!" Nancy yells again. They scramble back onto the sled. Rosy-cheeked, like Bouchers. Surely, no one ever had cheeks that particular color indoors. I never would have had children with cheeks this color if I'd married him, Nancy thinks. The man is sallow, even-toned. Even today, slightly out of breath in the cold, he looks as if no blood passes through his face.

∎

Nancy tries to spot his trench coat among the ski parkas, Irish fisherman's sweaters, and L. L. Bean earth-tone gear. It is his ankles that give him away. The suit pants ballooning over the rims of his socks make his silhouette different from everyone else's. Her eyes move up his ankles past his trench coat to his bare head. He has the same kind of bald spot Prince Charles has. It doesn't make her think of a man who is losing his hair. It makes her think of a man who is more manly for having something a woman can't have. She watches him as he stands at the peak of the sledding hill, hands still in his pockets, an island amid the jumping children, white-muzzled dogs, and bent parents.

Max and Goldie wait their turn. Max, the eldest, lies on the bottom of the sled and waits for Goldie before he takes off. Jeff gives them an extra push and they scream.

"Look out below!" Nancy calls to a struggling boy in dark blue. He is dragging his sled up the down path instead of the up path, which is lumpy and harder to navigate. The child is so overdressed his arms stand out from his body like a snowman's.

Nancy tunes her ears and separates Max and Goldie's screams from the other children's. Max paddles the snow with his hands to go faster. Then Goldie drops her feet to slow them down. Still, they make it beyond the end of the run, lengthening it by a yard or two. Nancy hopes the man sees how wonderful her children are. Jeff whoops, then runs down the hill to congratulate them.

In two steps, Nancy is next to the man. She stares straight ahead at her children and has no idea what she is going to say. Suddenly, "Do you still circle the movies you want to see in the *Times*?" comes out. He is silent. He looks straight ahead. Then, "What do you think?" he answers.

Still looking at the children, she speaks softly, almost without moving her lips. "I think you do."

■

He was an editor and lived the most censorious life she knew. He criticized things other people never thought about, labels on cans, the wording on menus, how people sat. He even criticized her syntax and her dreams. If she'd stayed with him, he would have criticized her into the ground. There would have been nothing left. Now married to a man less critical than she is, Nancy sees that she is to Jeff what this man would have been to her.

Nancy tries to find something else to say. Watching her family come up the hill makes her feel invulnerable. She could not have wished for a better way for him to see her, sculptural in her knitted hat, smiling at her beautiful children.

"The first time and the last time I ever had pressed duck was at your apartment," she blurts. The duck press. It was silver or chrome or stainless steel, polished like a mirror, expensive looking. He used it to squeeze the blood out of duck, which he served with homemade caramelized applesauce and braised leeks. Two other things she hasn't eaten since they parted. "How's the duck press?"

"I use it to crack walnuts." He snorts, the closest he ever comes to a laugh. She turns to him. She wants him to look at her but he doesn't. What if he liked what he saw? The relentless critic, the perfectionist. She might have liked herself better if she'd married him. It would have kept her on her toes. Jeff, on the other hand, loves her the way she is, loves her powerlessly. This man would have loved her conditionally, the way she loves Jeff. The question is, Does love mean more if you have to earn it?

"Tell me honestly. Do you ever think about me?" She is curious, not risking anything. Jeff and the children are halfway up the hill. Max throws a snowball. Jeff ducks. Goldie tries to wash Jeff's face with snow. He lets her. Jeff falls down and plays dead.

117

The kids hoot and dance around him. Nancy and the man watch.

"*Do* I or *did* I?" he asks.

"For a while I dreamed about you," Nancy says. "Once in a while I still do. It's always the same dream, but I don't have it often enough to call it 'recurrent.' " Nancy offers this, feeling generous. "Tell me," she says. "How many times do you have to have a dream before you can call it 'recurrent'?"

"Perhaps 'occasional' is the word you're looking for."

"Thank you," Nancy says as the children approach. She decides not to tell him how she feels when she wakes up from this dream. When he is cruel to her in the dream she wakes up longing to make things right. She wakes up liking Jeff less and wondering what she did wrong in the dream. She wakes up longing for the man who's been cruel to her. She wakes up wanting the wrong thing, a reckless dreamer.

"Mommy! Did you see how fast we went?" Max is breathless.

"Mommy! We went so far!" Goldie adds.

"Hurry!" Jeff says. "We're next!" He lies down on the sled first. Max gets on top of him, then Goldie gets on top of Max. The man watches as Nancy pushes them off. Jeff grunts and uses his hands like flippers.

Nancy speaks, her eyes on the sled. "In the dream, I come to your apartment. You seem glad to see me. You play the piano and sing for me. Then you walk me to the door and close it. I'm left outside your door. I'm left standing there without a coat."

"They say anything you dream can't come true."

"What do you think it means?"

"The meaning of dreams is meaningful only to the person who dreams them."

She wonders if he made that up, just thought of it, or if it's a quote. If he'd said, "She who dreameth the dream doth then become its mistress" or something like that, she might have taken a chance. She might have said, "Ah! Shakespeare!" But The meaning of dreams is meaningful only to the person who dreams them could be anyone. Freud. Delmore Schwartz. Borges.

"Do you live in the neighborhood?" Nancy looks at his feet. She can't find them. The snow is over the top of his socks.

"Yes," he says. She waits for him to ask if she lives in the neighborhood too, but he doesn't. They watch the sled stop. Jeff and the children roll off.

"Do you ever call me and hang up?" Nancy asks.

"Is that you who calls and hangs up all the time?" Finally he turns and looks at her. "Why do you do that, Nan? What possesses you?"

Nancy does not answer. Instead she imagines him alone in a dark, prewar apartment littered with *Times* TV pages, yellowed and flaking on the floor, draped over the back of the sofa, hanging on towel racks in the bathroom. The duck press, relegated to the bookshelves, separates his Paris-in-the-Thirties writers from the Southern Catholics. He still drinks wines with pedigrees, but he drinks them alone with food purchased from the gourmet takeout place across the street, this balding older editor who, dressed inappropriately, comes out in the snow to sample life firsthand. Looking at Jeff with the children, laughing, screaming, rosy, and wet, Nancy feels she has not made a mistake. She never could have pleased this man as much as Jeff pleases her when he pleases her.

■

Jeff pants up the hill. He is pulling Max and Goldie on the sled. His glasses are fogged over. The children take the next run without him.

"Put your arm around me," Nancy tells Jeff. A long, slim, down-covered arm rises and stretches over her shoulders, weighing heavy on them. She leans into Jeff and he curls his arm forward, a tropism. Although the editor's arm is fatter, Nancy knows she'd have to sense its weight. It would rest on her nonterritorially, as if resting on the arm of a chair. The three of them stand there, watching the children.

"Having fun?" Jeff asks Nancy.

She smiles at him. Can he see me through those glasses? she wonders.

Jeff smiles back.

"I'll warm you up when we get home," he says.

Then the tone of a scream changes and Goldie is lying face down in the snow. Her overdressed body looks like a pile of laundry. Jeff breaks into a run. Nancy follows, trying not to stumble. Oh please God, she thinks, then sees blood on the snow. It's the reddest blood she has ever seen, too red to be real. Jeff turns Goldie over. There is blood on her lower lip and chin. Nancy feels adrenaline carbonate her fingertips.

She bends down. She knows with Jeff there, all she has to do is kiss, lay hands, soothe. He will make the right decisions. No need to galvanize.

Goldie grins. "My wiggly came out!" she squeals. She runs her tongue along the fresh channel of her mouth. Fear crosses her face. "My wiggly! Where is it?"

Jeff, Nancy, and Max squat beside Goldie in the snow. They take off their mittens and probe around the blood spots. Goldie chomps a snowball to stop the bleeding.

"Look for a little hole," Nancy says. Jeff gives up last.

"I need my tooth!" Goldie whimpers. "I have to have my tooth!"

"The tooth fairy knows you lost your tooth," Nancy says. "The tooth fairy will make it up to you." She extends her legs and lifts Goldie onto her lap. She kisses Goldie's cheek. "The tooth fairy knows where every missing tooth is. All the teeth that have fallen out in playgrounds, in the ocean, on the beach. All the teeth that have swirled down bathtub drains and been swallowed during sleep. All the teeth that are lost at hockey games and football games and boxing matches. Do you think the tooth fairy would disappoint all those people?"

"You didn't say snow," Goldie says.

"Snow is the tooth fairy's favorite," Nancy says. "The tooth fairy gives snow special attention because teeth lost in snow are the hardest to find. Tomorrow," she continues, "when you wake up, look under your pillow and see what's there."

Goldie smiles up at Nancy the way Nancy then smiles up at Jeff. They drag the sled up together, mitten to mitten to mitten, Max leading the way.

At the top of the hill, Nancy sees the man is gone. She catches sight of his overflowing pants. He's pulling a sled with the stuffed blue child on it. A woman in high-heeled boots picks her way alongside of them. She too is dressed like someone who never goes out in the snow.

"Can't catch me!" Nancy yells, running toward them for a better look. The woman is wearing a red Hudson Bay blanket Nancy remembers from his bed. Black-cashmere-sweatered arms dangle from the shawl openings of the blanket, ending in long leather gloves. Despite its fullness, the woman's flounced Western skirt cannot hide that she is slim. The man looks down at the stuffed child and says something. The child hurls a snowball and he stands there, letting it hit him in the face.

■

On the way home, Nancy imagines that she is with the editor and that Jeff, whom she hasn't seen in fourteen years, passes them on the street. She imagines Jeff looking at the editor and thinking, So she married an older man. Fat, sour looking, losing his hair. Probably smokes cigars and wears English cut suits. Probably gives her a hard time. She imagines Jeff finding a way to tell her that sometimes he calls her and hangs up, just to hear her voice. That nothing is ever really over. Not ever. That he still dreams about her and would very much like to meet her for a drink.

RECKLESS DREAMER

■

Nancy, Jeff, Goldie, and Max stop in front of a flower store. They stare at overripe tulips and engorged daffodil buds behind the snow-lined window.

"Mom! Look! It's summer in there!" Goldie says.

"Can we have cocoa, Ma?" Max wants to know.

Nancy smiles at them. If I had stayed with him, she thinks, I would not have had these children. I might have had *other* children, but not *these*.

Max scrambles ahead of Nancy and flattens himself against a doorway. After a moment, his hand appears. Nancy can see his hand moving up and down. There's a snowball in it. The hand moves up and down, up and down, getting ready. An old terror she is still familiar with grips her. She takes a handful of snow from the hood of a car. She slows down, packing it. The children. It is not possible to imagine not having these children. There is no way to even think about it. It is something there is no vocabulary for. These children. She could never have had them with any man other than Jeff. Not these particular children. She walks slowly, giving Max a chance to make the first move. When he does, she compliments him on his aim and throws a long one, straight and swift, just high enough to sail over his head as he flies down the street.

———————

Mᵧ MOTHER'S KISS

My sister Sukey calls to tell me my mother wants to throw me a party for my fortieth birthday, six girls and no more at a fancy restaurant. Since I didn't go to my sister's fortieth birthday party, six girls and no more at a fancy restaurant, she tells me not to expect her at mine.

"Don't take it personally," she says. "But I'd have to be crazy to come to yours if you didn't come to mine."

∎

Sukey and I weren't talking then. The three of us, my mother, Sukey, and I, are never all on speaking terms at the same time. When my mother is angry at Sukey, she talks to Sukey through me. When my mother is angry at me, as she seems to be now, she talks to me through Sukey. Between us, we have explored every mathematical permutation of the number three. When who talks to whom, it means whom is not talking to whomever.

125

ALL IT TAKES

■

So why isn't Mother talking to me? Is it because I nodded to Aunt Betty at Uncle Al's funeral even though Aunt Betty failed to save Mother a good seat? Did Mother spot my super's daughter in the navy self-tie polyester blouse she gave me eight Christmases ago? Is it because on warm fall days I sometimes leave the house without wearing stockings? Maybe it's my hair. Maybe it's my walk. It could always be my posture. "If people were born perfect," Mother is fond of saying, "what would motivate them to improve?"

■

So I go through my phone book and try to pick out six best friends. There are lots of names in this phone book. The living, the dead. I can't bear to edit it. My best friend who committed suicide twelve years ago is in there. My grandparents. Big Lena, the house-keeper who told me I was her favorite. Jerry Lamb, whose idea of foreplay was to hang bookshelves for me or wash my car. Bea Redlicht, who used to make gift items out of gum wrappers. Bea hasn't answered her phone in four years. But the number isn't disconnected. It rings when I call. Who knows? Someday Bea might pick it up.

So I start with the A's. Enid Ashley. Enid is bright, but she embezzles her husband in a way I cannot accept. She has it worked out with the liquor store that when she orders a case of wine that's $5.99 a bottle, they bill her husband $10.99 a bottle and give her the difference, cash. She gloats, telling me this, while we sip coffee beneath the Ferdinand Botero her husband has given her for their anniversary. She sniggers, showing me a kitchen drawer brimming with corks. She says her husband, whom she refers to as The Patient, likes to finger these corks and say the price of cork is going up. Mara Turkel is another story. Mara buys two legs of lamb for $4.79 a pound, then returns one for cash. But unlike Enid, Mara embezzles to keep the peace. Experiences during her husband's early childhood have rendered him hopelessly tight. Unlike Enid who embezzles to put one over on The Patient, Mara embezzles out of love and concern. So I put Mara Turkel on my list:

1. Mara Turkel.

The B's are a wasteland. So, for that matter, are C, D, and E. There are two F's, though. One is a psychiatrist I helped through a messy divorce even though I now feel bound to her in the Oriental way one is bound to take responsibility for someone after saving their life. She is Beverly Fish, a noted analyst, who brings her own food to my house when she comes to dinner because she is afraid that if I cook something she is not fond of she will experience hunger. She keeps Twinkies and Maillard chocolate in her lap throughout the meal. She eats them in pinches and thinks no one notices. Beverly has told me, quite plainly, that I must never tell her a secret, because she feels bound to honor only the confidences of the couch. Beyond that, Beverly says, she cannot be held responsible. Which complicates things. If I invite her, it means I have to invite our mutual friend, Naomi Pinsky. For eleven years now Naomi has talked about how much she hates her job. And each time she talks about it, it's as if she's just discovered it. Once I said to her, "So, Naomi, what else is new? You've been hating that job a long time now."

"I most certainly have not!" she said. "What are you saying? I've loved my job until this minute!"

I don't want Naomi Pinsky hating her job all over my birthday party at a fancy restaurant so I put

2. Beverly Fish

on my list knowing full well Beverly will tell Naomi about the party, especially if I ask her not to, and that maybe this is what I really want. Then Naomi will stop being friends with me and I will stop being friends with Beverly for creating the rift between Naomi and me.

3. is easy. Frankie Footer, my oldest friend. I named her Frankie Footer in the tenth grade when she cried to me that she could not stand being Francine Futterman from Freeport one more minute. She hasn't legally changed her name to Frankie Footer, but it's in the local white pages that way. And it's what everyone except her mother calls her. Frankie's a good friend. We've been through a lot together. We once fell in love with the same man. Herb happened to be her boyfriend at the time. But when she introduced me to him, a primitive thing happened, the kind of thing you'd expect to see with a euglena. Frankie forgave me everything. So how could I not invite

her, even though I know she'll find a way to work what happened with Herb into the conversation. She always does.

H. I have to invite Danielle Haffey because we are always there for each other. We go to the funerals of each other's family members, even come in from weekends out of town for relatives we've never met. When we visit each other in the country, we bring covered dishes and work harder to make things nice than we do in our own homes. Also, Danielle is discreet. She's my only friend I feel safe complaining about my other friends to.

■

So where am I? I have Mara, Beverly, Frankie, and Danielle. Two to go. Because of various betrayals, I do not even consider Mona Jahn, Betty Kroll, Helena Lipsky, and Lois Levine, clumped together like the enemy in my phone book. Carol Moss is painting in a studio off the Rue du Cherche Midi this summer on the money she got from the city after the bus she was on crashed into a taxi and drove somebody else's sunglasses into her cheek. N. There's Ann Newberry. But Ann Newberry is nuts now. No job, no man, no money. She has borrowed from everyone while finding herself, even though all her friends have pleaded with her to find a job instead. Finding herself at forty-four. Even Moses was only lost for forty years.

■

So I fly through O, P, Q, and stop at Lisa Rein-
hardt. Lisa! Oh, Lisa! How jealous you will be of me
that my mother is throwing me a fortieth birthday party!
You will tell me she is manipulating me by allowing me
only six friends. Then you will ask me who else is on
my list and tell me why each person on it shouldn't be
there and how the restaurant has gone downhill. And
then you'll come late. Lisa! I could talk to you about
books till my throat charred. But how can I ask you to
my party when you try so hard to make me blue? And
what would you bring me for a present? A box of
cashews when you know I'm allergic to nuts? A small
hand tool from Odd Lot Trading? A deck of cards that
says "Compliments of American Airlines"? Oh, Lisa!
Sorry Lisa!

And sorry Annabelle Rafelson. Annabelle broke a
vase in my house and did not offer to pay for it. She
was, in fact, furious at me for leaving it on the mantel.
"How thoughtless of you to put it in such a vulnerable
place!" she tsk-tsked while I swept up the Imari, a
wedding gift from my great-grandmother. "Don't you
care about your guests?" Yes! I do! And you're not one
of them! Fare thee well, Annabelle!

•

S. Sue Simkin? The last time Sue invited me up to
her husband's showroom to get a new fall suit at cost,
he charged me retail. Same price as the stores. I'm
sorry if the Simkins are having a rough year. Everyone
knows the industry has been hard hit by imports from
Korea. But to charge a friend retail?

MY MOTHER'S KISS

∎

Mentally I wave, passing Mara Turkel in the T's. My U page, like my Q page, is pristine, except for United Housewrecking of Stamford. I put their number in my book years ago on the off chance that someday I might lead the kind of life that required, say, a pedestal sink or vintage porch. For reasons of self-preservation, I skip directly to Z. Arlene Zagoda cheated me in a land-development deal involving hydroponics in Nevada. Tomatoes were going to be grown on a man-made lake. It sounded good. Then the zoning fell through. Four hundred thousand seedlings scorched to death on the desert.

∎

I take count. Mara, Beverly, Frankie, and Danielle. Four. How can that be? How can I only have four friends good enough to invite to my fortieth birthday party? I'm busy all the time. All I do is see friends. Maybe when Mother told Sukey I could invite six, maybe Mother meant six including her and me. That's it. Subconsciously I understood this and that is why only four have made the cut. That must be it. I call Sukey just to check.

"Sukey?"

"I can't talk," she says. "I've got someone important on the other line."

Perhaps it is a doctor telling Sukey the results of a biopsy she has been brave enough not to tell me she underwent. Or the detective she has hired to tail her husband. Or her husband telling her he knows he is being tailed. Perhaps it is Mother.

■

I take a pint of Ben & Jerry's Dastardly Mash out of the freezer and work through it. I decide that when I reach the bottom of the container, when the lid is licked and the sides are scraped, I'll give Mother a buzz. I'll say, "Hello, Mother? . . . Mother? Are you there? Mother, I know you're not talking to me. Sukey told me. Is it my hair?"

"I don't wish to discuss it," she will say. Wish is her angry verb for want. Discuss is her angry verb for talk about.

■

I wade through the Mash and think, No. This should wait until I see her. Then I can tell her face to face that I love her and how much I appreciate that she wants to throw me a fortieth birthday party, six girls and no more at a fancy restaurant. But, I will tell her, I'm so sorry. I just couldn't get the list down to six. I care deeply about all my friends, I'll tell her. I love them and they love me. I'm sorry, Mother, I'll say. Really, I tried. And then when we say good-bye, she will brush my cheek with an air kiss so as not to smudge her lipstick and leave that smell on me that stays on my skin all day and lingers long after in my clothes. It's a smell like everything I've ever known. A smell like a three-family tag sale on the first good Saturday in May. A smell that's sweet and sour, flowery and dank, cool and warm, clean and dusty, fleshy and artificial, the smell of my youth, a layered scent that starts with her soap, then her creams, then her powders, then her make-up, then her cologne, then her perfume, plus the incalculable something my mother's own self brings to this assortment.

THE YELLOW BANANA

"Seven men died making this bridge," Roy said as they swerved onto the Manhattan side of the ramp.

"You don't know that."

"Actually," Roy said, "it was seven and a half."

"What do you mean, 'half'?" May turned toward him in her seat.

"Well, part of one guy's still down there." He could afford to be silent now. He liked when he had information she wanted. He liked her having to ask.

"What do you mean?"

"Well, when they were pouring the pylons, somebody got sucked in with the cement. Part of him's still down there."

"What did they do with the rest of the man?"

"They took him to Our Lady of the Sacred Tear Hospital."

"You made that up."

"His name was . . . Wilbur McGillicuddy."

"There is no Our Lady of the Sacred Tear Hospital," she said, bluffing.

They rode in silence, suspended over the East River by necklaces of light.

"You know," May said as they approached Brooklyn, "there's a club in Holland for people who love this bridge. The Brooklyn Bridge Club. They meet and they talk about the Brooklyn Bridge. Then once a year they come over and look at it. That's it. That's the whole club."

"I don't get it," Roy said. "They come all the way here just to look at the bridge? How long can you look at a bridge? Half an hour and I bet somebody says, 'Okay, we've seen the bridge. Let's eat.'"

■

They drove down the ramp and entered Brooklyn. May thought the borough looked darker than Manhattan. There was no street life. The buildings were old and squat. The streets were named after people she had never heard of, obscure explorers and New World financiers.

"I wonder if they buried your uncle with his leg," May said.

Roy looked at her as if she'd gone crazy. "What are you talking about?"

"Did they or didn't they bury your uncle with his leg?"

"They get rid of it at the time of surgery. You think they save it?"

"Oh, I don't mean his *real* leg. I mean his artificial leg. Did they put it on him in the casket or not?"

"How should I know. Jesus." He took a turn on two wheels. "But why should they? He won't be needing it."

"You never know. They buried Tut with all that stuff. They thought he'd need it in the afterlife."

"Our people don't believe in the afterlife."

"Well, wouldn't it be hard for the pallbearers to carry a coffin with uneven weight distribution?"

He didn't answer her.

"How would it look in the coffin? There would be this, well, this sag. It wouldn't look right. I mean, it would look uneven."

"But everyone who came to the funeral knew he only had one leg."

"That's not the point," May said.

He decided not to ask her what the point was. Whatever the point was, it would be hypothesis. He preferred the inarguable. He liked questions with real answers. He knew if he kept silent there was a chance she'd get distracted.

"What do they do with the leg after surgery," she said.

"Limbs are usually burned unless you request them to be buried."

"I'm serious," May said.

"So am I."

"No, really."

What, he wondered, did she *think* they did with them?

"You really want to know?"

"Yeah."

"They sell them to McDonald's."

137

■

He was pretty sure he was lost now. It was that turn off Atlantic Avenue. Suddenly the stores had gone from upholsterers and children's clothes to pig-part emporiums and voodoo parlors.

"Are we lost?" May asked.

"No." Roy answered so quickly she knew they were. "Look for something that says Flatbush Avenue, I think."

They turned into a side street and he pushed the master lock button. All the doors clicked and she felt uneasy from needing the extra security. What if a gang leapt out of the dark with lead pipes? Would he have the sense to run them over? What if someone was pretending their car broke down? Would he know enough to pass them by?

"Are you angry I wanted to see Ettie?"

"No," Roy said.

"I mean, I think your uncle would have liked it. No matter what your family thinks of her, he loved her. Really, Roy. I think it would have pleased him you're going. Your family treats her so badly. At least you're not ignoring her. She was an active part of your childhood. It only seems right to say you're sorry."

"She's a pain in the ass," Roy said.

"Well, she took care of Sussman a long time. She was his nurse, practically."

"She killed him."

"What do you mean?"

"She talked him out of a pacemaker. She convinced him the surgery would kill him. Instead, his heart killed him."

"Well, God." May's voice caught. "I hope I never have to make that decision for you."

"Me too," he said and smiled at her.

He liked the way she looked in her fox coat. So unconcerned about the cold. Not like the women in his family. They wore dark wool coats over buttoned-up cardigans supplemented by knitted scarves and sad hats, hats that even new had looked defeated. Their hands were always busy clutching fabric around their throats, protecting their pocketbooks, shielding their breasts, pushing those sad hats down. But even on the coldest days May never wore a hat. She let the wind flail her long curly hair into a tangle that beat against her eyes. She laughed when her hair got in her eyes and she never closed her coat. A long strand on pearls flew out in front of her, wagging like a metronome in time hips. "Here comes May! Here comes May!" A silk blouse was all that stood between her and the cold the women in his family clutched against. She never carried a bag. Just stuffed change and credit cards in her pockets.

"Sit close to me," he said.

May undid her seat belt and slid over. He put his arm around her shoulders and let his hand slide down her breast. You could argue that the feel of a hard nipple was even nicer through silk. He wondered if she was reacting to him or the cold.

139

"Would you mind concentrating on the road?" she said. "I don't want to die in Brooklyn. Besides, I think we're lost."

"No. This looks familiar."

"We haven't been here in five years." She paused. "You know what? I think this is a Yellow Banana."

"What's that?" Roy asked.

"A Yellow Banana is when something doesn't turn out the way you expect it to."

"Give me an example."

"Remember when Jo Ann recommended that Cuban restaurant and we went there on our anniversary and you got a Band-Aid in your soup and I got food poisoning from my batido? That's a Yellow Banana. Remember when you paid a hundred and forty dollars for closed-circuit seats to a fight and the man got knocked out in the first round? That's a Yellow Banana. Remember when we waited six months to see *Cats* then couldn't understand the words? Looking for a place in Brooklyn that you have no directions for on a dark night in January, that could very well be a Yellow Banana too."

"You mean like the time the Gilchrists told us to meet them at a Chinese restaurant on Eighty-third and Broadway and there was no Chinese restaurant on Eighty-third and Broadway?"

"That's a Yellow Banana. That's right."

"Why do you call it a Yellow Banana?"

"Because a Yellow Banana doesn't mean what you'd expect it to."

THE YELLOW BANANA

"You mean a Yellow Banana does not mean a banana that's yellow?"

"You got it."

"Look for a spot," Roy said. "This is it."

He pulled into a metered space. May got out of the car and ran into the building. She knew it would take him three or four minutes to check out all the parking signs and make sure he wouldn't be towed or ticketed. She plunged her hands deep into her pockets and studied her neck in the lobby mirror. How could she complain about him not turning his socks right side out before putting them in the hamper when he was willing to read parking signs on sub-zero nights in Brooklyn? He entered the lobby red-cheeked and preoccupied. She held his arm while they rode up in the elevator. They rang Ettie's bell. The hallway was dark and smelled of fermented garbage.

"Who's there?" Ettie's voice said.

"May and Roy," Roy answered.

A police bolt jolted up from the floor. A lock turned and a chain jiggled.

"All right." They heard Ettie's voice from inside. "All right, all right already."

Roy and May stood in the foyer and let their eyes get used to the light. In addition to ceiling fixtures, there were floor lamps and table lamps everywhere. All the shades had been removed and the penumbrae from the bulbs made it difficult to find a place to rest their eyes. Ettie, dressed in black, looked Roy up and down.

141

"So," she said. "You came. Let me take your coats."

"That's okay," Roy said as they walked toward the living room. "We'll just throw them down."

He let his eyes take in the room. Sussman's chair was still where it had been five years ago, surrounded by two floor lamps and a table lamp. His leg was leaning up against the side. Roy was struck by how unbionic it looked. There was no attempt to make it look real either. It was as if the prosthetist had no point of view. The artificial limb was a combination of woods, dark yet faded, like the hull of a sunken ship. It was held together with leather and screws. Perhaps Sussman had ordered the economy model. That would have been in character, Roy thought. Sussman always prided himself on never living better than any man who worked for him.

Roy draped the coats over the back of Sussman's chair, beside the leg, and sat down on a small fringed wing chair. May squirmed on a settee, working her way around the lumps beneath the slipcover.

"We were so terribly sorry—" she started to say. Ettie interrupted her.

"You never came. He was so sick. We could have used you."

"What?" May said.

"How come you never came? Every day he'd ask me, 'Where's Roy? Why doesn't he call?' "

May watched Roy, wondering what he'd say. She had asked him the same thing many times.

"I want to remember him the way he used to be. I want to remember him strong," Roy had always answered.

"Well, what about me? When I'm old and sick will you leave me so you can remember me the way you want to?

"You'll just have to wait and see," he'd always say.

"He took you to the circus, Roy." Ettie shook her head. "He taught you the Charleston. Whenever there was a fight, he'd say, 'I'll get three seats. One for me. One for you. One for Roy.' "

May watched, waiting.

"It was terrible, terrible," Ettie continued. "And you never came. You never called."

"I didn't know he was that sick." Roy said. "No one told me."

"The last time you saw him, he was in the hospital."

"Yeah, but I thought he was better. No one called to tell me he was still sick. Why didn't you call me? If he was that sick, you should have called me."

"We didn't want to bother you. You should have called us. It's unbelievable you didn't call. Want a drink?"

Roy shook his head.

"How about her?" Ettie pointed to May.

"No, thank you," May replied. "We haven't eaten yet. We're going out to dinner. Would you like to join us?"

"Our people stay home for a week," Ettie said. "Come on." She turned to Roy. "Have a drink. I want you to have a drink. You took all this trouble to come see me. Now have a drink."

Ettie stood up and began working her way around the room. She circled the rim of the Oriental rug. May and Roy noticed a bottle of Scotch on the floor, underneath a lamp table. "I know I have a bottle in this room. I just saw a bottle here yesterday." Ettie let her hand drift over the bookcases and chair backs as if she was feeling for the Scotch. She was stooped over, shorter than the last time May had seen her. Her hair, once dyed black, was stained purplish brown. She wore it in an upsweep, all the brittle ends trapped at attention under a net, frazzled old lady hairs shaped into a hair fez longer than her face. She scuffled over the carpet in deliberately cut slippers, warped bones peeking out of scissored slits.

"I know it's here. I know I have a bottle of Scotch. Here." She picked a can off the coffee table and held it in May's face. "Have a hard candy." May put her hand in. The candies were unwrapped and sticky.

"I better not," May said, withdrawing her hand. "We're going to eat soon."

"Go ahead!" Ettie waved the can under May's nose. "Who's counting calories?"

May reached in, extracting a small green waffle. She and Roy watched Ettie wander around the room while they stared at the bottle of Scotch under the table.

"You could have called," she said, lifting cushions off chairs. "Christ, what's a phone call?"

"Do you have a Kleenex," May asked.

"Why do you want a Kleenex?" Ettie shuffled over to May.

"I'm crying."

"There's a box next to you. Help yourself."

May blew her nose and spit the green waffle into the Kleenex. Ettie watched her.

"You like the candy?" she asked.

"Delicious."

"You think so?"

May nodded.

"Well, don't take any more. It'll ruin your appetite."

Ettie walked toward the entrance of the living room and for the first time May noticed the presence of a supermarket shopping cart. It was loaded with crumpled shopping bags, newspapers, and empty bottles.

"I know it's here somewhere." Ettie began taking things out of the cart and putting them on the rug. "You know, Sussman never knew why you didn't call. You should have called."

"In defense of Roy," May said, "I think you should know. No one ever told him Sussman was so sick. All this has come as a real shock to Roy."

Ettie turned to Roy and pointed to May. "What did she say?"

"Well now, you've got to start taking care of yourself," Roy said.

Ettie exhaled loudly and slumped in a chair. She seemed to have given up looking for the Scotch.

"Yeah? You think so? I haven't had a vacation in years. Since he got sick. I've let myself slide. Look at me." She turned to May. "Am I a wreck or what?"

May studied Ettie's face. She had lost weight and her skin hung in dewlaps crushed with wrinkles. The whites of her eyes were yellow. Some kind of surgery had been done on one of the lower lids. It looked as if a bite had been taken out of it. Her old teeth were brown. Her new teeth were white. The uppers went to the left, the lowers to the right. At the corners of her mouth two whitish deposits had collected. May imagined they were equal parts Milk of Magnesia and Breakstone's sour cream. She wondered if looking like this was in her cards.

"I think a vacation would do you good," May said.

"Why don't you go south?" Roy suggested. "Take a few days. Go to Miami."

"Miami?" Ettie asked.

"Yeah. Miami. That's a great idea."

"So you think I should go to Miami?"

She began petting her hair, searching the rim of the net, pushing, tucking. "I used to look a lot better. You know that, Roy. I used to look good. Why didn't you call, Roy? You could have helped."

Roy stood up.

"You can't leave without a drink. Have a piece of candy. You want a drink?"

Roy got their coats. He lingered for a moment behind Sussman's chair. May watched him let his hand gently touch the leg. She wondered if he was remembering something nice, like the Sundays Sussman took him to see the Walrus Woman at Coney Island. Or Sussman buying him his first ice cream soda at Schrafft's then teaching him how to drink it through a straw. They followed Ettie to the door. It was odd knowing you were seeing someone for the last time. How rare that was. She would never see Ettie again. Most times people don't know the last time they're seeing someone. May's eyes stopped on the console by the front door. She noticed a glossy travel brochure for a round-the-world cruise on the QE2.

"We're so sorry," May said.

"You could have called."

"Let us know if we can do anything," Roy said. He led May down the hall to the elevator.

■

In the car May waited for him to say something. She waited then finally said, "She took good care of him for a long time."

"Sussman didn't die," Roy said. "He escaped."

When they got to a light, Roy looked out the window at a street sign. He put on his directional.

"We are, at this very minute, two blocks from what is, quite possibly, the best seafood restaurant in all of Brooklyn. Nay, New York."

She didn't say anything. She sat looking quietly out the window. They drove that way until Roy shot through a yellow light, made a sharp right, and pulled into a spot.

"Know what they're famous for here?" he asked May.

147

"What?"

"Clam bellies."

"Clam bellies?"

"Clam bellies."

May remembered to smile. "Clam bellies," she said. "And what do they do with the rest of the clam?"

Rules and Laws

Y o! Goldring!"
There he is, sitting Indian style on the floor.

"Goldring, no?"

It's him, surrounded by two-year-olds, explaining the limited defense mechanisms of the toad genus *Bufo*.

"Aren't you Alex Goldring from Great Neck North?"

He had been the best at everything then. Best wrestler. Best debater. Best at throwing an M&M up in the air and catching it in his mouth. Friday nights standing on the girls' side of the gymnasium, I would pray that he would ask me to dance. *I'll never do blank again if Goldring asks me to dance.* Or *I'll always do blank if Goldring asks me to dance.* I'd stare at him hard then look away, artfully shy, when he looked back. I'd nod and shout, "Yo! Goldring!" the way everyone did when he passed by. I also tried laughing like Rima in *Green Mansions. She laughed like the tinkling of silver bells.* I'd shake my red hair as if a fly had crawled in my ear. But girls had no control of their

---

destinies then. We had to wait to be asked. And
Goldring never asked me. He only asked the short
girls. I never thought the five or six inches that separated us were meaningful. I thought more in terms of
Napoleon and Josephine, Sonny and Cher. If I could
find him attractive, couldn't he find me attractive?

■

Goldring blinks.

"It's me," I say. "Honey Lazar from high school.
Honey Lazar Blum now, actually."

He cocks his head.

"We went to high school together," I say.

He rises from the floor without using his hands.
He is still short. And he still holds his dark head down
so when he looks at me, the tops of his irises are
buried in his upper lids, the whites shimmering below.
Now I realize, after seeing many stigmata paintings,
that this is partly responsible for his aura of intensity.

"Sorry to interrupt," I say. It is the first day of
school for my first-born. His too, it turns out. We
shake hands. "Guess I've changed a lot, huh?"

He raises his left eyebrow and right shoulder,
evoking with economy his old easy grace.

So I introduce Alex to Norm and Alex introduces
us to Ginger and it's a shock. While Norm looks
nothing like Goldring, Ginger could be my double.
Like me, she has bright red bushy hair. Like me, she
does not have pierced ears. Like me, she has eyes that
make you feel like a liar no matter what color you write
on your driver's license. But unlike me, she is wearing

red. Red dress, red handbag, red shoes. I am speech-
less. The cardinal rule for redheads is "Never Wear
Red." I learned "Never Wear Red" before I learned
"Look Both Ways Before Crossing." It's the first thing I
remember my mother saying to me. "Never Wear Red"
was more important than "Never Write Anything to a Boy
You Wouldn't Want His Mother to See," "Never Order
Hamburger in a Chinese Restaurant," and "In a Strange
Bathroom Always Feather Your Nest."

■

Goldring! After all these years! I wait a couple of
weeks, then invite them for dinner. Then the Goldrings
invite us for dinner. Then we sign up for a concert
series and by summer we are sharing a house. It is at
this house that I notice Ginger seems to have no idea
what any of the rules for redheads are. She wears Bain
de Soleil instead of PABA 25. She sits there on the
beach, courting skin disaster, in a faded red cotton
string bikini. She does not even cover her hair. I
decide one day, while we watch our children parallel
play in the sand, to find out what, exactly, is going on.
  "So Ginger," I say. "How come you always wear
red? I mean, you don't know about the rule?"
  "Honey," she says. (I hate my name because I
never know if people know it's my name or they're just
calling me "honey.") "Of course I know about the rule.
Every redhead knows about the rule. That's why I
always wear red."
  Her favorite book is *The Red and the Black*. Her
living room furniture is covered in red damask trimmed

with red silk fringe. When we go shopping, she heads straight for the red. When she finds an item she likes, she buys in multiples. If the red pants are well cut, she buys two pairs. Flaming red patent Pilgrim flats with outsized silver buckles so captivate her, she buys all three pairs the store has in 9½ narrow and asks them to send to the factory for more.

If Goldring minds, he doesn't show it. He saves his fights for when he can win: The best way to light a charcoal grill, The exact location of a particular star, How to tell if a fish is really fresh, The best place to buy the best goat cheese at the best price. He is silent on the usual fight subjects: movies, politics, whose turn to wash, whose to dry. Sometimes, out of boredom, Ginger rises to the occasion. They go at each other in a terrifying way, breathing through their teeth. Norm and I watch them, feeling close at these moments. We hold hands and bask in our mutual respect for each other. We would never fight in public.

It is also at this house that Goldring seems to be giving me a lot of attention. Usually, I get the full focus of it. Sometimes I make a stab at integrating the conversation: "Hey, Norm! Goldring says Great Danes have the shortest life expectancy of any kind of dog!" or "Hey, Ginger! Goldring says he knows for a fact McDonald's put sugar on their French fries!" or "Hey, everybody! Guess what! Goldring says Freud had an undescended testicle!" But I am the only one who ever responds. I am the only one who seems to care. And I give up trying to involve Norm and Ginger not only from lack of success but from flattery as well. It is an honor for me to be the sole beneficiary of Goldring's attention. Even when I know he is wrong, I say nothing. His mind is so keen, his authority so great, I don't care. I don't want to break his speed.

∎

Back in the city, a month or so later, Ginger tells Goldring he is welcome to stay, but she is going to date. Fine, he says, I'll date too. And it seems to work. They divide the refrigerator, get separate phones, take their own things to the dry cleaners. Until Ginger gets tired of Goldring's acceptance of the situation and throws him out.

"Ginger," I warn her. "Don't throw him out. Some other girl will snap him up."

"So I should keep him because somebody else might want him?"

"Ginger, don't you know about the rule? 'Never throw out dirty dishwater till you have clean'?"

"I've got a Hotpoint," she says.

∎

It doesn't work, staying friends with both halves of a couple once they separate. Even the couples that call you up and tell you please not to feel you have to choose. You still wind up choosing, in this case by attrition. Goldring never returns our calls. Ginger does. She even invites us to her Valentine's Day party. The apartment is filled with red anemones. She serves red caviar canapés, red snapper in tomato sauce, red pepper and radicchio salad, and meringues filled with raspberry sorbet. Saying good night at the door, Ginger asks me what I hear from Goldring.

"Nothing," I say, head down.

"Don't feel bad," Ginger says with such concern the corners of my mouth twitch. "That's just Goldring. He forgets people. That's what Goldring's like."

·

I assume I will live a life without Goldring. Then there he is. It's Goldring at the Food Emporium, banging the soda can reclamation machine with his fist.

"Yo! Goldring!"

He fixes me with his moody eyes. "This fucking machine," he says. It is riveting. "I put in six fucking cans and only got a fucking quarter." He unfolds his hand and there it is.

"Look, Goldring," I tell him. "Tell the manager. You don't have to take that."

I watch Goldring seek out the manager. I watch him point to the machine. He waves his hands. He shows his quarter. The manager reaches under his apron and gives Goldring a nickel from his own pocket. Then Goldring heads for the exit.

"So long, Goldring!" I shout. He stops at the door. He looks at me.

"Hey, hon," he says. "Want a ride home?"

Goldring leafs through *The National Enquirer*, immersing himself in the cover story, "COW GIVES BIRTH TO HUMAN," while I check out. Then, struggling under the weight of two grocery bags, I follow him to his car, a low-slung reptilian model, the kind men get when they leave their wives.

"The trunk releases from the interior," he says, leaning in. He pulls something and the trunk pops open. He stashes the groceries then slides in beside me. "The suspension is superior to every other sports car on the road. I have quadrophonic sound." He pulls a Benzie box out from under the seat and plugs it in. He rams a cassette into the black hole. Dag Nasty blasts through the interior. My eardrums hum. "The controls for the sound system can be operated from the passenger's seat as well as the driver's." He flashes me a smile and pats me on the knee. My legs fall open. "So what's with Norm?" Goldring asks.

"He's okay," I say. "What's with Ginger?"

"How the hell should I know."

He leaves rubber pulling out of the spot and we are silent as he heads toward my building. He stops in front of the awning. We stare at a bag lady screening garbage.

"So," I say, after a while.

Goldring does not pick up on it. I reach for the door handle. I pump it up and down. Nothing happens.

"Trapped!" Goldring says and starts to snort. "You can't get out unless I release you." He flicks his fingernail against a knob with a picture of a knob on it. "I'm going to keep you here, car captive. 'COUPLE LIVE IN CAR.' We move to alternate sides of the street until your groceries run out."

"Then what?" I say, squirming in my seat, getting into the spirit of the thing.

ALL IT TAKES

Goldring is silent. His shoulders sag. I've never seen him at a loss for words before. His possible disintegration is too horrible to contemplate. I try to remake my question as if it had really been a statement.

"Then what I'd like to do is make a thermos of coffee in case we get thirsty. Want some coffee? A nice cup of coffee, Goldring?"

"I've got a better idea." Goldring brightens. "I'll make the coffee and you can see my new place."

If Ginger and Goldring were still living together, I wouldn't think twice about saying yes. But what, I wonder, is the rule for going up to a man's apartment when that man is separated from your friend even if you were friends with that man first and only came to know the woman later? Nothing seems to apply. I fall back on instinct.

∎

Goldring has chosen a family building to live in, one owned and managed by his uncle's company. We ride a mahogany-paneled elevator up to the sixth floor. Sunlight streams in from the park. I watch the children playing soccer across the street. No noise is heard through Goldring's double-hung windows.

I follow him into the kitchen. The counter is lined with an electric coffee apparatus, an electric can opener, a microwave, a toaster-broiler, a popcorn popper, an electric juicer, and a chrome espresso machine with a spread-winged eagle on top. It looks like a small appliance store. Goldring fills two Styrofoam cups with tap water and drops a teaspoon of instant coffee into each of them. Then he puts the cups in the microwave and presses 10. Casually, I cover my ovaries and wait for the bell.

We sit, sipping hot instant coffee, not having much to say. I am still waiting for Goldring to do something, waiting for him to ask.

"Hey!" He slaps his leg. "Want to see something unbelievable?"

I follow him into the bedroom. There is a queen size bed with a Mexican bedspread over it. The TV has three machines on top. Two large Idaho potatoes with wire probes in them sit in a plastic dish.

"Goldring," I say. "What's with the potatoes?"

"That's a two-potato clock," he tells me. "In case of a blackout. The bimetallic probes convert the potatoes' natural energy into low voltage. It's as accurate as my Rolex Submariner."

His phone begins to blink.

"Excuse me." Goldring walks over to the phone and presses a few buttons. He listens, then writes something down with a magnetic pen that sticks to the side of the phone.

"That phone light tells me when I have messages on my tape. Incoming numbers show up here. Also, I can talk on this phone without even touching it. Here," he says, patting the bed. "Watch."

I sit next to him. He presses one button then hangs up the phone. I hear a series of electronic beeps, then Ginger's voice is saying hello.

157

"Hello?"

"Hi, hon! It's me," Goldring says. "I just wanted to show Honey how the phone works."

"She's *there*?"

"We ran into each other at the Food Emporium!" I shout.

"How's Jenny?" Goldring asks.

"She's fine. You can pick her up at ten tomorrow but make sure you have her back by seven."

"Over and out," Goldring says. There are two clicks and a beep and the phone is quiet. "Know what my favorite thing to do here is?"

"What?"

He grabs a remote control panel and turns on the TV. A green basketball court appears. He starts to play. "The better I get, the tougher the computer gets," he says. "Just when you think you're getting good, it really gets tough."

I watch Goldring play.

"Got him! Jesus! Dammit! Did you see that?"

Goldring is giving it all he's got. By half time, he is losing 64–60. He takes off his sweater. His T-shirt is dark around the armholes. I get a whiff of him that takes me back to our high school gym.

When it is over, 132–129 Goldring, he lies back on the bed and closes his eyes. His breathing returns to normal. He seems to have fallen asleep. I tiptoe toward the door.

"Where you going?" Goldring says, patting the bed. I sit where he pats. The bed starts to shake.

"It has massage control as well as hospital bed

positions." He presses a button. A motor engages. The head and foot of the bed rise, forming a U, engulfing us.

The phone whirrs. Goldring leans over me. "Yes?" he says to the air at large.

"Goldring?" A male voice fills the room. "I've got a line on a chronometer that can tell the time in eight countries."

Goldring tries to sit up. "You're kidding." He unwedges his hand from where it is trapped behind my knee. I glance at the potatoes. Goldring notices. "Where are you?" he says. "Are you someplace I can call you back?" He shoots me a look. "Can I call you back, say, in fifteen minutes?"

"Fifteen," the man says and hangs up.

"Honey," Goldring says, switching his phone tape to ON. Then he is looking at me, kneading my upper arm. "Honey, Honey, Honey. Honey. Honey and Ginger. What is it with me and girls named after food?"

"Seventeen years, Goldring," I say, as his hand begins to pump my breast. "We've known each other seventeen years. Seventeen plus."

"Right," he says. "High school. We went to the same high school. I remember. Want the bed on or off?"

"Off and down," I say.

He presses the appropriate buttons, then rolls on top of me. He plows my legs open with his.

"Wait," I say. I pull my sneakers off and bend over to tuck them by the bed. They bump into a pair of flaming red ones, patent leather Pilgrim flats with outsized silver buckles. I stare at them, my head upside down. "So does Ginger come here much or what?" I ask. My voice sounds as if it is being filtered through water.

I hear his zipper. Then he answers. "Nah," he says.

" 'Nah' as in sometimes? Or 'Nah' as in never?"

" 'Nah' as in never."

I raise my head and rest it next to his.

■

Sometimes you go through with something because you think you don't want to but you really do. Other times you go through with something because you think you want to, but you really don't. Then there are the times you go through with something simply because it is inevitable. And at those times what you go through happens with the kind of velocity that is described at length in the laws of physics. It is that same thrust that, when a car stops short, keeps you moving forward regardless, over the steering wheel, clear through the windshield, and out onto the hood.

ALL IT TAKES

Dear Miss O'Keeffe,
    Although I am familiar with most of your work, I have never felt my spirits soar as they . . .

Dear Georgia O'Keeffe,
    I've probably spent a third of my waking life looking at pictures. Still, nothing prepared me for . . .

Georgia O'Keeffe!
    Wow! Lake George with Crows! *Wow!*

    Lucy and Simon head back to their hotel room after doing the East Wing of the National Gallery. They are in this cab together in Washington heading back to their hotel room because Federbush has suggested a change of scene. Now Lucy wonders whether Federbush meant a change of scene together or a change of scene apart. It hadn't occurred to them to ask. Did marriage counselors ever suggest separations? They must. They must try

lots of things. When Federbush suggested a change of
scene, it sounded as if he had lots of things for them to
try. If one didn't work, they could try another. It was
like fixing a car when you don't know what's wrong
with it. First you try one thing, then another, then
another. All it takes is finding the right thing and the
car works. Now Lucy wonders. Being in Washington
with Simon when one lives in New York with Simon is
a change of scene, but what does it take you away from
besides walls, work, dishes, and the phone?

Lake George with Crows, Lucy thinks. *Georgia
O'Keeffe*. A woman whose life was connected, one part
flowing into the next. Even her home. Lucy remembers
the pictures she once saw in a decorating magazine.
There was no furniture, just shapes, Georgia O'Keeffe
shapes, growing out of the floor and walls. Shapes to sit
on, shapes to eat on, shapes to talk over. Lucy thinks,
Georgia O'Keeffe's life was whole, of a piece. I am
Lucy, Mother of Jake. Lucy, Wife of Simon. Lucy,
Daughter of Dorothy and Lester. Lucy, Assistant Profes-
sor of Art History. Where is Lucy, the Real Lucy?
Georgia O'Keeffe was only Georgia O'Keeffe.

■

Lucy studies the transaction between cabdriver
and husband.

"I don't think you tipped that man enough," she
tells Simon in the lobby.

"What do you mean? I gave him a dollar twenty-five."

Simon shifts his weight from foot to foot. Even
deep in Federbush's brown armchairs, Simon gives the

impression of an athlete on the bench waiting for a signal from the coach.

"What do you mean?"

"You gave him *twenty-five*," Lucy says. "The cab fare was four twenty-five and you gave him four fifty."

"He said *three* twenty-five." Simon lays his slender hand on Lucy's shoulder. She stares at it, noting that his college ring has slipped so that the large yellow stone is palm side. "Honey, the fare was three twenty-five and by giving him four fifty I gave him a dollar and a quarter tip."

"He had holes in his gloves," Lucy says, head down.

"I know he had holes in his gloves. That's why I gave him a dollar and a quarter tip."

They take the elevator up to eleven and, smelling smoke, return to the lobby.

"There's smoke, or at least the smell of smoke, on the eleventh floor of the hotel," Simon tells the concierge, a delicate Indian girl in a wilted black suit. Her purple eyelids quiver.

"I shall call security," she says, sliding a walkie-talkie out of her breast pocket by the aerial.

Simon grabs Lucy's hand. "Let's see what happens. Want to see what happens? We can have a drink and watch."

He pulls Lucy toward the Kon Tiki Lounge.

"It's too early to drink. It isn't even lunchtime."

Lucy and Simon sit on backless leather benches facing an alley of elevator doors. Lucy settles in, easing her black knitted skirt so it won't stretch. Nothing happens.

"There could be a fire going on in this hotel right while we're sitting here, and no one is panicking," Lucy says. She shakes her head. Her excitable hair itches the side of Simon's face. He scratches under his nose. They sniff. Then they hear fire engines. Men in canvas coats and oversize fire hats, men younger than Lucy and Simon, burst into the lobby. Lucy and Simon watch them race to the elevators. The men stand there looking up, staring at the DOWN arrows. They stand there, holding axes and folded hoses, along with the other people waiting to go up.

"I thought you were always supposed to take the stairs when there's a fire," Lucy says. "You're never supposed to take an elevator when there's a fire."

"They want to make sure there *is* a fire."

Lucy and Simon watch an elevator engulf firemen.

"Look!" Simon points to the elevator nearest them. "That elevator isn't moving. Watch. Some people get on and realize it right away. But there's a lady in a tweed suit with bedroom slippers on who went in there a while ago and she still hasn't come out."

"Come on."

"I mean it. She's in there. She's been in there at least five minutes studying her convention brochure."

Lucy walks over to the elevator. It is empty except for a heavyset woman in a tweed suit and bedroom slippers.

"This elevator isn't working," Lucy tells the woman.

ALL IT TAKES

"What I need to know is, are the Wives of the Corporate Giving Program meeting in the Jefferson Suite or the Madison Room?"

"I'm sorry, I'm not with the convention," Lucy says, backing out of the elevator.

"Well then what the hell are you doing in the elevator? Jesus Christ." The lady goes back to her brochure.

An elevator door opens, disgorging wives and firemen. Simon grabs a fireman's arm.

"What's the story?" Simon says.

"Somebody burned a napkin in the ice cube dispenser."

"Is it safe to go up to room 1108?"

"Safe as it'll ever be," the fireman says. He smiles and tips his hat to Lucy. She smiles back.

"Let's go upstairs," Simon says to her. "It'll be nice after all this excitement."

Lucy recalls hearing once that firemen always make love after a fire. That after a fire is the only time they really like it. They are no good on vacations, or Saturday nights after a movie, or when the children are visiting grandparents. But after a fire, they love it. After a fire, it reaffirms life. It tells them they are still alive.

"I don't know," Lucy says, looking down. "It's early. I think I want to go back to the museum. I could have stayed there longer."

Simon makes a hook out of his first finger and jacks up Lucy's chin. "You can only see so much," he says. "After the first half hour, you might as well go for coffee. You know that, Luce."

"I don't know. I could have stayed there longer."

"I'll be waiting," Simon says, stepping into the elevator.

Dear Miss O'Keeffe,
I too would like to live in a house where there is nothing I can get along without . . .

Georgia O'Keeffe:
I'll be brief . . .

Georgia, Georgia,
No peace I've found since seeing Lake George with Crows *. . .*

In the museum Lucy finds *Lake George with Crows* right away. It surprises her that she likes it just as much as she had earlier in the day. It surprises her that she hasn't exaggerated how good it is in her mind. She stares at the painting. She feels as if she is being sucked into the painting, a part of its world. She can feel the breeze the crows are hitching a ride on. She can smell the lake. She can feel fall coming. And she can see Georgia O'Keeffe, splendid, painting in the nude by an open window. Lucy's eyes swirl over the painting, seeing it in its entirety, without a focal point. She thinks of Georgia O'Keeffe blending into her life in Abiquiu, form into form, everything unified, everything flowing without a break into the next thing. The hills flowing into the adobe walls that flowed into the adobe table that flowed into Georgia O'Keeffe's elbow resting on it. Georgia O'Keeffe's life flowed into Georgia O'Keeffe's house and came out in her painting. Without a focal point. Everything had equal importance. Everything was part of the whole. Not like the ruby brooch of Madame Moitessier that Ingres painted hot white. The eye went right to it and everything else fell away. Not like the glow over Cecil George Newton's head in Tissot's *Hide and Seek*.

Lucy's eyes keep roaming, over the mountains, down the trees, through the water. Her breasts inflate from excitement. She feels hungry. She walks down the stairs and boards the moving sidewalk. She follows the cafeteria signs. For lunch she chooses all healthy things. A side order of stewed mushrooms, mashed acorn squash, yogurt, and blueberry pie. She sits down at a table for four, facing the waterfall. The waterfall makes just enough noise to drown out most of the conversation in the cafeteria, with the exception of a Southern couple refining their travel arrangements. Lucy thinks the woman's voice has a quality to it that could make people crazy, a subliminal whine. Lucy looks at the husband. She wants to see if his face shows signs of wear. But he appears to be interested in what his wife is saying.

Lucy stares at her tray and after a moment decides to remove her plates. As she does, she notices that the texture of the tray is the same as the ripples of the water in the waterfall she is facing. And the food she has chosen has the same colors as *Lake George with Crows*. Yogurt clouds. Mashed acorn squash trees. Blueberry mountains. Fried mushroom tree trunks. And the lake in *Lake George with Crows* is the water of the waterfall. Eating the squash, Lucy thinks that the only thing missing is a cup of black coffee crows.

Lucy considers getting coffee. But what if somebody takes her seat and either eats or throws out her blueberry pie? She spots a uniformed tray dumper.

"Oh, miss? Miss?"

A pretty South American woman with a gray cloth in her hand looks up. Lucy wonders why so few people who work in Washington come from Washington. Everyone she meets is from somewhere else.

"Miss," Lucy says politely. "I want some coffee, but—"

Before Lucy can explain about her table and the cup, the woman interrupts. "You got to get your own, lady," she says, turning toward the garbage dolly.

Lucy thinks she could eat the pie plain, without coffee, if she has to. But then another uniformed tray dumper comes by eyeing Lucy's tray and empty dishes.

"You can take it." Lucy smiles at the dark, balding woman. "I'd like to get a cup of coffee, but I'm afraid I'll lose—"

"Coffee over there," the lady says, taking a swipe at Lucy's table with a foul-smelling towel.

The coffee will probably be cold anyway, Lucy thinks.

A narrow-hipped tray dumper of Oriental descent floats past.

"I'm afraid I'll lose my seat!" Lucy blurts.

"You no lose seat," the lady says kindly. "*Your* seat." She puts a reassuring hand on Lucy's shoulder, leaving four gray circles on the front of Lucy's white silk blouse. "*Your* seat," the lady explains. "You stay. You eat. Food good."

Lucy eats the pie and stares at the waterfall. The crust is airy but the berries are hard and oversweetened. She relinquishes her dishes to a tray dumper and sets out to find *Lake George with Crows* again. She wants to know if she still likes it as much as she did the other two times.

Dear Miss O'Keeffe,
  I'm so tired of making things possible for other people. . . .

Miss O'Keeffe—
  Is it true your earliest memory was of light? Mine was too. . . .

Miss O'Keeffe,
  No two lives could be more different . . .

Lucy pauses in front of the moving sidewalk, waits for the right moment, then lurches on. She is so anxious to see the painting again that at the end of the moving sidewalk she forgets to slow down and stumbles off the conveyor belt, crashing her knee into the Tennessee marble floor, a pale desert pink. She limps up the stairs and finds herself in the new wing of the National Gallery, right in the middle of a tour.

A bookish docent with a beard is holding one of his elbows and talking about the triangle. How the triangle is used as a leitmotif for the new building.

ALL IT TAKES

Lucy looks around and sees that everything in the new wing is broken into triangles, the floors, the walls, the ceiling, all triangles linked at their points.

The docent switches elbows. It is a stance Lucy associates with academics. The held elbow, along with the pipe, the boyish bouncing gait. Lucy listens.

"The architect of the old wing was John Russell Pope. The architect of the new wing was I. M. Pei. Now," the man becomes excited, "people always ask me, 'Is that I. M. *Pay* or I. M. *Pie*?' Good question!" Lucy doesn't realize she has groaned until she sees the man staring at her. He clears his throat. "The answer is," he continues, "it *depends*. Mr. Pei is from Canton, where Pei is pronounced *pay*. But if he were in Italy, it would be pronounced *pie*."

Lucy studies the man's face carefully. He appears to think he is telling the truth even though *ei* in Italian is pronounced *ay*, and Pei would be *pay* in Italian as well as Cantonese. Lucy listens to see if she can catch him again. The crowd of people on the tour are attentive. But the man is in error. Lucy stalks his words, waiting.

"This tapestry was designed especially for this wall by Joan Miró," the man continues smoothly. "First Miró painted a small painting of the design and then he gave it to Royo to execute. It took Royo . . . *a full year* to complete and weighs more than two tons."

"Excuse me," Lucy interrupts, raising a finger. The man nods at her. "If Miró gave Royo a painting to make the wall hanging from, who decided on the texture of the piece? Miró? Or Royo?"

170

ALL IT TAKES

The man drums his fingers on the elbow he is holding.

"That's a good question," he says. He squeezes the elbow. "I don't really know the answer to that."

Lucy smiles.

"No. Wait a minute," the man says. "Miró gave the painting to Royo and then visited Royo every six weeks to check the progress on the wall hanging. Uh that's what happened."

Lucy can tell he is making it up. She watches the people listening to him. A crowd of Washington tourists, ruddy-faced men with cameras trying to look interested as if looking interested could grow into being interested, clumps of gray-haired gray-coated women, a pair of blue-jeaned lovers with legs of equal length, and a few wives hoping for a detail interesting enough to pass on to their husbands over dinner. They shift their feet and catch each other's eyes. They watch as Lucy tries to discredit a man who abuses his authority by not telling the truth.

"Both the new wing and the old wing were built on top of the old Tiber Creek," the man is saying. "I. M. Pei literally *floated* this building on a six-foot slab of concrete so that in case of flood or drought, the building can rise and fall on its slab as a whole."

This sounds wrong to Lucy. She clears her throat.

"What did John Russell Pope do when he built the old wing?" she asks. "To protect it from the water, I mean."

"Good question!" the man says. "And the answer is . . . *nothing!*"

ALL IT TAKES

"So what happens to the old building if there's a flood or drought?" Lucy persists.

"Well," the man is kneading both elbows. "Last year, it just so happens, part of the pediment actually fell off. Luckily, no one was hurt."

"How do you know it was from the water table that the pediment fell off?"

The man flexes his nostrils. The crowd turns to him, waiting. He has dropped his elbows and is pulling his fingers. The crowd parts as he takes a step toward Lucy. Lucy glances down at her watch, then bolts. "Nevermind!" she calls over her shoulder. "It's okay!"

Running, Lucy tries to find the old wing.

"No running," a guard calls after her. Finally she is back on the moving sidewalk that connects the two buildings. She takes it to the cafeteria and buys a cup of coffee. It is cold, and the only milk they have is a nondairy creamer with no natural ingredients.

Dear Miss O'Keeffe,

How blessed you were to be able to paint the things you had no words for. . . .

Dear Miss O'Keeffe,

How interesting that you started out making big things small and wound up making small things big. I like the way you ran things into things. . . .

Dear Miss O'Keeffe,

I'm having a little problem with my husband and life in general. What appeals to me about your

ALL IT TAKES

*work at this particular time is the way it connected
to you, the way you lived, and through that to
me. . . .*

Lucy studies the oil slick on her coffee and abandons the cup to the tray dumper. She boards the moving sidewalk, hoping it will take her to the old wing. At the end of the belt she sees an old wooden door and knows she is in the right place. She tries to find *Lake George with Crows*. She walks through the Impressionists that leads to the Post-Impressionists and hopes that if the rooms follow art history they will lead to Georgia O'Keeffe. But the next room is dominated by David's portrait of Napoleon in his study and she is back with the Neoclassicists. She retraces her footsteps through the Impressionists and finds herself in a bright room full of Fragonards, dappled light teeming through trees and cotton candy ladies on swings. The paintings make Lucy feel queasy. They look too eager to please. Lucy wants Georgia O'Keeffe. She turns to a guard.

"Where can I find *Lake George with Crows*?" she says.

"Do you live in Washington, miss?" he asks with a West Indian accent.

Lucy finds her way to the rotunda, hoping to retrace the steps she took earlier in the day with Simon. But the rotunda is perfectly symmetrical and Lucy cannot tell which way to go. There are no clues. She heads left.

173

"Excuse me," she asks another guard. "Do you know where I can find Georgia O'Keeffe?"

"Does she work here?" the guard says with a burr on the *r*'s.

"She's a painter," Lucy explains. "She did a painting called *Lake George with Crows* and it's here somewhere, only I can't find it."

"Ah, yes," says the man. "Many tourists tell me that. They tell me when they come to the National Gallery, they can't find their favorite painting. But you see," he says, "that is because many of our paintings are on loan."

"But I just saw the painting this morning," Lucy says.

"And you want to see it again?" The guard frowns. He takes a step toward Lucy.

"Nevermind. Thanks anyway." Lucy turns to go.

"Why do you want to see it again?" the guard calls after her.

Lucy enters another room and is stopped by a Degas called *Madame Camus*. It is painted in shades of terra cotta. Lucy feels herself getting excited. She has never seen this Degas before. It is a Degas painted at just about the time when Degas became interested in photography. He was seeing Madame Camus with the camera's eye. He was putting everything in the picture he would have seen through the viewfinder. He was cropping it the way a camera would. As Lucy studies the painting, she notices a white triangle has bled through the right side. It's a bit of underpainting she hadn't noticed at first. Lucy's eyes stay on the white triangle. When she tears her eyes off the triangle, they slide right back to it. It's not Degas's fault his paint has oxidized. It's not his fault his paint has grown translucent. Still, Lucy misses the continuity of *Lake George with Crows*. She is tired of *Madame Camus* and Degas's premeditated spontaneity.

Someone touches her arm.

"It's time to go now, miss," The guard speaks with a Spanish accent. "We're closing now."

Lucy takes a cab back to the hotel. The fare is three twenty-five. She hands the driver four fifty and walks into the lobby. When she gets off the elevator she sniffs the air for the smell of smoke. She follows the corridor to 1108 and sticks her key in the door. She turns the knob, but the door is chained on the inside.

"I'm coming." She hears Simon hoist himself off the bed. "Where the hell were you?"

"I told you I was going to the museum." Lucy puts her handbag down on the bureau and catches a look at herself in the mirror.

"All day?" Simon says. In the mirror she sees him walk up behind her and put his hands on her shoulders. "You spent all day at the museum?"

"And what did you do?" Lucy stoops out from under his hands, ducking his arms. The room is small. When she stops moving, he puts his hands back on her shoulders.

"I waited for you," he says softly, sweetly. "I spent all day waiting for you."

175

ALL IT TAKES

Dear Miss O'Keeffe,

*Do you suppose there's an Abiquiu for everyone?
What I mean is, a right place? . . .*

Dear Georgia O'Keeffe,

*Did you really hate those summers, all that family
round the table? . . .*

Dear Miss O'Keeffe,

*All right. You made me see things the way you saw
them. Now what? . . .*

"Are you hungry?" Simon yawns.

"I had lunch at the museum."

"It's dinnertime now. We could order up."

"That sounds nice." Lucy lifts Simon's hand off
her stomach as if she is handling a live lobster. Simon
rolls away from her and extracts the room service menu
from beneath the phone.

"What do you want?" he asks.

"I don't know." Lucy bites her lip.

"What do you feel like?"

"I don't know." She struggles to sound calm.

"Well, what *don't* you feel like? We can start from
there."

"I don't know," she whispers. "I don't know."

"Do you *not* feel like Dover Sole Veronique? Do
you *not* feel like Poulet au Crème Moutarde? Do you *not*
feel like Tournedos Rosini?"

"All right. Read it to me."

ALL IT TAKES

∎

Simon takes a shower before dinner. Lucy curls up in the bed and stares out the window. He has told her that if they part, she won't have anyone to tell her she is beautiful and smart. Which means, of course, that he does not really think she is beautiful and smart. No matter, she decides. A life circumscribed by pain notices only pleasure. Pleasure is what stands out and leaves its mark. Pleasures become milestones. And with that in mind, Lucy looks forward to the Roast Rack of Lamb Persillé for two and the broad expanse of Simon's hard hairless chest as he strides out of the shower with a towel around his waist, his hair a scramble of wet black worms.

Dear Miss O'Keeffe,
Is it true you broke Stieglitz's heart? . . .

Dear Miss O'Keeffe,
I too am most interested in the holes in the bones. What you see through them. Negative space. What's missing becomes more important than what's there. . . .

Dear Miss O'Keeffe,
What can you tell me? What do you know? What does it take? . . .

177

SYZYGY

He just nibbled Goo-Goo clusters and stared at me. He stared without reservation, as if the two-way mirror was still between us. Occasionally he asked questions of his assistant brand managers. Questions that led them to discover what was important without being told. But the whole time, he stared at me. That was Chattanooga, four years ago. We were doing focus groups on an experimental detergent with a built-in deodorant. The agency needed to know if women thought clean-*looking* clothes could smell bad. In other words, could something look clean and still be dirty? How did you know if a brown towel was really clean if you couldn't see the dirt on it when it was dirty? Was there a target audience for smell as proof of clean?

For three days I probed the women of Chattanooga's deepest laundry disappointments, six groups a day, 9:00 A.M. to 9:00 P.M. I grieved with them over the shadows of their stains. I mourned the ink blots on their men's shirt pockets. I used my gift for making people believe I am just like they are. It's a gift that convinces strangers I'm on their side.

In between groups, I joined the clients in the room behind the two-way mirror and chatted with the assistant brand managers. He stared from his perch on the side of a table. At the end of each day the room was filled with Goo-Goo Cluster wrappers, mashed soda cans, Styrofoam cups, and deserted sandwich halves. Each night we returned to the hotel, exhausted and wired from boredom and coffee. On the last night everyone shook hands in the lobby. Even though I knew I had done a good job, I couldn't sleep. The hotel had a pool. I decided I would swim myself to sleep. The pool was round and warm. I swam its diameter. Back and forth, back and forth, touching the rim of the pool, turn, touch, turn. Then I reached out and my fingers were on his thigh. I looked up.

"What is it," I said. "What's the matter?"

And he said, "I can't bear how happy I am to be in this pool with you. I will tell you right now that this is the happiest I have ever been in my life and ever hope to be."

■

Today's the first time I'm seeing him since he moved in with his trainer four months ago. First he calls and says, Hey, I'm going to be in town on the seventh. If Judith can't come, can we get together? Then on the sixth he calls and says, Hey, guess what? Judith can't come. Then on the seventh he comes.

SYZYGY

"Hey," he says, waving from the steps of the Met. "I'm so glad I get to see you." He smiles at me the way parents do on visiting day at camp.

Right away I notice something's different. Anytime I see him after a long time I'm numb with observations: He cut his hair. He lost weight. I still love him. He still loves me. Is that a new shirt? What's with the limp?

"You look different," I tell him, touching the tip of my shoe to the tip of his.

"I do?" he says.

"It's your right eyebrow," I say.

Then he tells me. His right eyebrow is growing. It's growing like crazy. It started three months ago. Just like that. "I actually have to cut it with scissors," he says. "I have to trim it."

He tells me he knows when to trim it because he has to push it out of the way to read. He tells me that and then he laughs. I can't bring myself to mention that his right eyebrow is getting white too. It's not easy seeing your ex-lover grow old on one side. If we were still together, that eyebrow might be young.

He looks me over. "Your hair," he says. "It's longer."

"Hair grows an average of .00000001 miles an hour," I tell him.

"Well," he says, picking one out of my mouth, grazing my lips and my cheek. "What do you want to do?"

I decide for the first time not to say Whatever you want to do. I know if I say Whatever you want to do, he'll say Well why not go to the museum? But I'm tired of walking around museums with him. I'm tired of us bumping into each other maybe on purpose, maybe not. Maybe accidentally brushing hands or hooking pinkies. We're friends now. He lives with this muscle-ridden Judith. He picked his fitness trainer over me, even though he's told me he doesn't love her as much as he loved me when he loved me. I try to believe what he says. Maybe he doesn't like love.

"I don't want to go to the museum," I say.

"You don't?"

"I've had it with museums. I'm museumed out." Then I get an idea. "Want to see the Lower East Side?"

What he says next he says as if I have suddenly become a difficult woman. "What's on the Lower East Side?" he says.

"That's where my ancestors lived when they came to this country. I want you to see where they lived. Want to see where they lived?"

■

We've never taken a subway together. But it seems like a good idea to go no frills. It seems like a good idea to do it steerage, the way my ancestors did it. So I treat him to a token and we head downtown.

"I've never seen that before," he says as a battered woman holding a battered-woman sign makes her way through the subway car. He stretches into his front pocket for change and I realize I have no idea what stop to get off at. Bleecker isn't the Lower East Side, it's the Village. So we pass Bleecker and get off at Canal. But Canal isn't the Lower East Side either. Canal is Chinatown. The streets are packed. All we can do is shuffle.

"Hang onto your wallet, okay?" I say as we pass windows filled with rows of copper-colored ducks. They're hung by the feet. Their eyes are open. I stare at his reflection in the window while he stares at the ducks. I see a man thirtyish, with Kennedy hair, a fat bottom lip, and arms that press against the sleeves of his button-down shirt. A man four inches taller than the woman he is standing next to. She wears her hair in a carefully messed-up way and understands unstructured clothes. She leans on the man so lightly it could be accidental. Her face has the look it must have had yesterday when a stranger stopped her in the street and said, Miss? Are you okay?

They walk down a block where everyone is selling fish. There are fish enough to make you finally understand that yes, the earth really is three-quarters covered with water. One vendor has fish flapping in a basket. There's no water in this basket, but these fish are alive. They're gasping. Their mouths are open so wide you can see into their stomachs. They're drowning on air. They have whiskers at the sides of their mouths, whiskers like stray hairs. We stare at the fish.

"What a way to die," I say.

"Are we almost there?" he keeps asking, like a kid in a car.

We see vegetables we've never seen before. Mountains of them, green, white, purple. We ask what a thing that looks like an octopus is.

"Sha-fong," the man says.

"Let's get one of these!" I point to something folded in brown leaves tied with grass. It looks gift wrapped. People all around us are eating them. I have no idea what it is, but I'm hoping he'll admire my spontaneity, compare me to Judith and find her dull.

But "You don't know how it's made," he says. "How do you know it's safe?"

We press toward Delancey. Someone eating cannoli steps on my foot. Cannoli. I look both ways. Sure enough, it's the San Gennaro Festival. We're in Chinatown *and* Little Italy. It is possible to have one foot in Chinatown and one foot in Little Italy at the same time.

"Want a cannoli?" I say. "Sausage and peppers?"

"Do you really want all that grease?"

This is the third time today I have felt I'm becoming troublesome, that I am bringing him something less than pleasure. This man who finds pleasure where other people never dream of looking. This man who hoists his pants with the sense of a job well done. I see the outer edges of his love curl like raw liver on a hot skillet. All I ever wanted from a man was to feel good when I heard his key in the door.

We cross the street and we're in Chinatown again. We keep heading east. The people thin out. We are almost alone. Then we find ourselves at an intersection that has six or seven cross streets. The buildings are low. It is filled with light. You can hear the wind. No one's around. It's like that scene from *On the Beach* when, against Gregory Peck's advice, a sailor abandons the sub to go back to his hometown even though he knows everyone is dead from radiation. Everyone is dead and he'll die too. But he takes a raft to shore anyway and everything is still there, exactly the way it was when he left. Fallen bikes on the sidewalk, wash hanging on the line. Only there are no people. Screen doors flapping, wind chimes chiming. No one.

Newspapers whirl around our feet. It's an odd wind, a wind like a whisk. It blows things in circles. Maybe it's the syzygy. The paper said today that the earth, the sun, and the moon are in rare alignment. That this happens once in a blue moon. And because of this rare alignment, we can expect an extra gravitational pull. Maybe that's what this is. We lean into it and cross the intersection.

"We're getting closer," I say, noting Spanish dads with little girls in pink tulle dresses and men in yarmulkes with ladies in thick stockings. "You're about to see my origins."

We cross Bowery, then Allen, and when we get to Orchard, I know we're close.

"We're almost there," I say as we pass shoe stores, underwear stores, complete-reading-glasses-in-30-minutes stores, discount men's pants. I brush into him and say, "My great-grandfather walked down this street." We make a right on Delancey, cross, and in two blocks we're at Eighty-eight. Eighty-eight Delancey Street, where it all began. I wouldn't be standing here in front of this building with my ex-lover from Macon if what happened here hadn't happened. My grandfather was conceived here, right in this building. It's a discount appliance store now. But once my great-grandmother and great-grandfather made love here, in this building. Once they held each other and pressed together, belly to belly, sweat into sweat, legs between legs. These people I do not know. They pressed together with nothing between them and my father's father was born. Then my father. Then me.

We walk inside. I watch him comparison shop cassette recorders. My ex-lover from Macon comparison shopping cassette recorders in the place my grandfather was born. He does it with his usual intensity, the same way he stared at me during the focus groups in Chattanooga. It's the kind of intensity that makes a man better looking than he is. I watch him in the overhead shoplifter's mirror. Then I look around. The walls are Sheetrocked. The floor is covered with red-and-black squares of linoleum. I am standing in the building my great-grandmother and great-grandfather started the American chapter of our family in. What would they have made of him? Of us? Would they have understood? Understood what?

I walk over to where he is fondling phone jacks and say, "We are standing in the place my family started."

He puts the jacks down. He looks at me. I don't know what I want him to say.

"What can I say?" he says.

"We could eat the same food they ate. We could go to Russ & Daughters and get lox on a bagel with vegetable cream cheese."

SYZYGY

But he doesn't want Lower East Side food either. So we grab a cab and head uptown and on the way he tells me about this guy on the radio in Macon. Mr. Answer. He can answer anything.

"Someone wrote in asking if Catherine the Great really did die the way everybody thinks she did," he says.

"Well, she did, didn't she?"

"No. Actually she didn't."

Then he tells me one that really shocks me.

"Swamis swallow rags to clean out their intestines," he says. "The rag goes down into the stomach and after a while, they pull it back out."

"I never thought of that as being something you should clean," I say. "But what do I know? I only just found out you're supposed to clean the tops of doors."

■

At the first good not too expensive place, I ask the driver to stop. I know what he's starving for in Macon. He's starving for what he thinks people are eating in New York. Salads with hot lardons, fresh buffalo mozzarella, crab cakes, radicchio, blackened anything. Regional foods from any region but here. So we stop at a place that has all that, even though what sings to me, what I hunger for most these days, is what I imagine he's eating with jocky Judith down in Macon—cheesy grits, honey baked ham, whatever collards are, and coconut cake so light it shakes. Once in the supermarket, I found myself stroking yams.

ALL IT TAKES

I leave half my polenta in cream sauce for him. I watch him savor his chicken in purée of roasted black pepper con funghi. Then he says, Are you leaving that? and I tell him my polenta has his name on it. He beams, a happy man. He raises his fork, smiles, and puts it in his mouth. He closes his eyes. He hums. He makes it last. He eats like he makes love. I can see him as a child chewing the paper after he finished the cupcake. And even though he's not fat, he always gets the bread basket refilled twice. The second time the waiter never brings butter. But that doesn't stop him. He just says, ever so politely, May we have more butter when you get a chance?

These are the things that churn my heart. But I know it's only a question of time before they get on Judith's hyperkinetic nerves. Unless she loves him enough, slow eating and thirds on bread are going to do them in. I know this because he told me she gets angry when he calls the CD a Victrola and makes a sucking noise against the roof of her mouth when he rocks in a chair that's not a rocker. If her phone doesn't ring for an hour, she asks him to call her from his line to make sure hers is working. Once he found his pocket marimba in the garbage.

"So did she get her divorce yet?" I ask, watching him mop sauce with his bread thirds.

"I don't know," he says. "She doesn't want to talk about it. How are things with you?"

I want to tell him that the stone is missing from my husband's ring. I want to tell him that I noticed the stone was gone two weeks ago. The blue stone from his

188

college ring. How long can my husband go without seeing it? How long can a man go without noticing his own hand?

"I don't know," I say. "I don't want to talk about it."

And then I start to laugh. It isn't the kind of laugh that goes down well in a public place. I do my best. I put my head close to the table and cover my face with my hands. I laugh directly into my hands. I grab a napkin and press it over my mouth. But just when I think I have it under control, I start laughing again, worse than before. I am gasping for air. It's the kind of laughing that happens at funerals and places where you know you can't laugh. I keep trying to stop. I can't. Finally I do.

He looks hurt. "What's so funny?" he says.

"You're surrounded by women who don't want to talk." I want to feel sorry for him. But he's one of those men who get loved all the time. A man who gets loved easily. It's not that he doesn't deserve it. He listens when women talk, just like on the soaps. He listens and shows pleasure.

Our knuckles meet mid-table. I try to figure out why I feel so bad. Both of us are unsure of the future. We're equal there. But he's trying to see if things are going to work out with this Judith. And I'm trying to see if things are not going to work out with my husband. Both of us are unsure. But we're unsure in opposite directions. Maybe that's it.

"Look." He leans forward. "I never loved anybody like I loved you."

"Same here," I say.

ALL IT TAKES

"It was so new for you," he says. "It made it new for me."

I study his face. It's all right. He's not saying I was a novelty.

"Well," I say. "That's qualitative. But I'm glad you told me."

■

When the last lick of sauce is gone, when there isn't one sesame seed left in the bread basket, he sits back in his chair and puts his hands on the sides of his stomach. We split the check. I leave the waiter an extra two dollars like I always do because of the bread.

We head uptown and walk till the rain. It starts randomly, like air conditioners dripping on our heads. Then it picks up and we turn into a bus shelter. In the bus shelter there is a poster of a woman in a yellow bathing suit offering a man in a swimming pool a glass of low-end Scotch. She's wearing one of those new bathing suits, cut high at the thigh. This bathing suit is cut so high at the thigh that it makes the model's crotch seem as long as a penis. It bulges too. It bulges too much. I take a closer look. It's been retouched to do that.

"What's wrong with this picture?" I ask him.

His eyes roam the poster. After a while he comes up with "Drinking and swimming don't mix?"

"No."

"They're too upscale for the target?"

"No," I say. "Give up? Look between her legs."

190

SYZYGY

He glances down. Then he moves his head right into the poster.

"Good grief," he says. "They must be going for the cross-dresser market."

What I say next I say like a tentative soup eater. I blow on it first, then give it a moment. Still it burns my lips. "It's a way of making a man comfortable with a woman," I say. "For me the message is Men like women who are like men."

We study the poster till the bus comes. We sit side by side. My whole side is against his. Shoulder, arm, hip, thigh, knee, calf, foot. I try to remember the last time we made love. It was more than a year ago. I try to remember if I knew it was the last time then, and if I believe it was the last time now. That is, will this be the most we'll ever touch again? We ride side against side, staring at the rain. A strange feeling creeps over me. I feel suspended. I feel weightless. I feel like a banana coin in jello. I am aware of his body pressing into mine, and yet I feel alone. Perhaps this is our syzygy. A rare alignment of shoulder, arm, hip, thigh, knee, calf, foot that results in increased feelings of aloneness.

"Want to know how Catherine the Great died?" he whispers. I feel his warm breath through my hair.

"Mmmmmmm."

"In St. Petersburg. A heart attack on the toilet."

Just like all my grandma's friends, I think but don't say anything.

When I notice we are only two stops from my stop I say, "Call me next week?"

"Sure," he says.

"And I'll call you too," I say.

He is thoughtful. He is silent. He is troubled. "Look," he says. "Sometimes she listens when I turn on my tape." Then he adds, "So if you do call, watch your mouth. Judith might hear."

"Watch your mouth? Did you say Watch your mouth? You said Watch your mouth, didn't you."

Maybe in Macon, Watch your mouth is an okay thing to say. Maybe down south Watch your mouth is as genteel as "I'd be beholden to you if you could find it in your heart to behave in your usual exquisitely discreet fashion." Maybe Watch your mouth feels different when you hear it down south.

Watch yo' mouth.

Watch yo' mouf.

Watch yo' mouf, you sweet, sweet thang, ya.

∎

The bus is at my stop. The doors are closing. "Getting off!" I shout, running to the front. The driver opens the doors again.

I watch the bus until enough cars pull behind it so all I can see is its roof. Not until then do I realize I have not said good-bye to him. We've never forgotten to say good-bye. So as soon as I get home I call and leave a message on his tape.

"Hi!" I say to his answering machine. "It's me. I'm going to watch my mouth just like you told me. I'm doing it right now. It's really hard though because my nose gets in the way. I *can* see my upper lip though.

SYZYGY

But it doesn't look like a lip because I'm seeing it from the top. I'm looking *down* on it, instead of straight on. It means crossing my eyes, watching my mouth. Really. Try it. You have to cross your eyes to watch your mouth. So I can't stay on too long. But I want you to know, and anyone else who might be listening, that I really am watching my mouth. I'm really trying hard. Okay. I better hang up now. You wouldn't believe how much watching your mouth hurts your eyes."

I hang up the phone and head for the kitchen. Frozen fried chicken. Preheat the oven. Peas and potatoes. People have to eat. Something is over. Something is ending. This is it then. The beginning of something else.

COME FLY WITH ME

Your father's too fat for a vacation," Ma says.

"Hmmmmmm," I hum, making a big deal out of cutting my meat.

"He's too fat to get into his tennis shorts. They don't make tennis shorts big enough for your father. Even the fat man stores."

I glance at Dad. He's chewing in earnest, rising to the challenge of a ligament. He's working on that roast beef as if he does it for a living. "Is this a gorgeous roast beef?" Ma turns to him.

"Fern. I think I need another piece." Ketchup squeezes out of the corners of Dad's mouth, bright as tiny Christmas tree lights. His head looks like a pea on top of an egg.

"Another piece?" Ma raises her eyebrows. "Have *two*, darling."

Dad passes his plate.

"A week at a spa." Ma turns to me. "I signed us up. They guarantee you six pounds a week. Harold . . ."

Dad looks up from his loaded fork to Ma and back, then finally puts the fork down. "Do you have anything to wear *to* the spa?"

"Excuse me." I carry my plate into the kitchen. When I come back to the table, I stand behind Dad. I drop my hands onto his shoulders, close to his neck, and kiss it where you can see the holes the hairs come out of.

"You still look like Paul Newman, Daddy. Doesn't he look like Paul Newman, Ma?"

"Paul Newman never weighed an ounce over one sixty. Not in his life," Ma says.

"The gray fox is turning into a white fox," Dad says, his speech slurred by roast beef.

•

Upstairs Dick watches college football on the old bed in my new bedroom. It's the guest room now. The ruffles, pink butterflies, and scrolled white furniture are gone. In their place Ma has put chrome, tweed, and a purple silk lily in a matte black vase.

"I can't stand it," I tell Dick.

"Did you save me some dinner?" The light of the TV plays over his face.

"She's so mean to him. The way she talks."

"Watch this guy. This guy's going to get MVP."

"Do you think he's fat?"

"Did you see that pass?"

"I want to go home." I stand in front of the TV. Dick moves his head to the right.

COME FLY WITH ME

"Here." Dick makes room for me on the bed.

"Say, 'Aw, poor baby,' " I say.

He pats the top of my head then squeezes it as the ball is fumbled. I decide to prove that I am more important to Dick than college football. I click to MUTE and shove the zapper down the waistband of my pants. He takes his time looking for it.

"Is it *here*?" he says. "Is it *here*? Hey . . . maybe it's . . . up *here*."

■

I like making love on the bed I used to wonder what making love was like on. The trouble is the new chrome headboard hits the wall. The floor is safer but the kilim scratches. Standing doesn't work. We're the wrong heights. And when we start out on a chair we always wind up on the bed.

" 'You're going to the moon, Alice,' " he says, " 'To the mo-o-o-n,' " as the headboard taps our message loud and clear.

Tap.

Tap, tap.

Tap, tap, BANG! Tap, tap, BANG! Tap, tap, BANG! BANG! BANG!

"Yes," I whisper to Dick, rolling him on top of me then rolling me on top of him as if we're rolling down a hill together. It's a move I picked up from *Betty Blue*. "Yes."

■

ALL IT TAKES

"I don't want to hurt your feelings, Ellen," Ma says. "I'm going to say this as carefully as I can. Why do you wear that thing?"

"It's a piano shawl, Ma."

"I'll give you fifty dollars, *seventy-five*, if you promise me you'll spend it on a nice robe."

I've come down for breakfast because there's no other way to get coffee. Upstairs, Dick is still asleep, his round brown shoulders gift wrapped in the sheets. Whenever I feel I can't say no again, Dick drives me home to Northport and we stay the night. While I'm thinking about how to put more time between these trips, Ma introduces her favorite topic. Distancing. Distancing is what happens when your daughter no longer confides in you. Distancing is what happens when your daughter no longer starts sentences with, Guess what happened to me today? Or, I have a problem. Or, What do you think Ma, huh? Distancing is the erosion of a relationship. It is marked by extreme politeness. It starts with crumbs, like having to get off the phone in a hurry for a flawless reason and ends in hunks like not being able to show up for a birthday or Thanksgiving. Ma's friends complain they are losing their daughters to distancing. It is taking them like the diphtheria of old. Daughters are dropping like flies. Daughters mothers brought through painful ear infections, acidosis, nocturnal coughs, wart removal, cold sores, growing pains, braces, dateless New Year's Eves, vegetarianism, term papers, teachers with grudges, finals, doctorates, unwanted hair, nerves, bad haircuts, bad apartments, bad roommates, bad marriages,

---

furniture selection, betrayals by men, betrayals by women, self-betrayals, the tyranny of the menses, wisdom tooth extractions, the heartbreak of acne. Now these daughters, Ma tells me, no longer confide. Their lives are sealed like cornerstones. They won't even argue.

"Distancing," I say. "Hmmmmmm."

" 'Hmmmm! Hmmmm! Hmmmm!' " Ma imitates. She pours the coffee. Her hair is flawless. It doesn't look like hair but it does look flawless. She is wearing her morning duster, a floral number with a mandarin collar that almost but doesn't quite hide the empty skin under her chin. Where does that come from? What happened to what used to fill it? Is that my inheritance?

"I'm not distancing, Ma," I say.

"What?" she says. "What did you say?"

I am saved by Dick, freshly showered, loping down the stairs. He skips the last three steps vaulting over the banister. He kisses the top of my head. Then he walks over to Ma and raises his hand, threatening to pat her coif. It is a fragile thing. Spray cracks.

"Oh Dick don't." She ducks.

"Why do you make the best coffee in the world, Fern?"

"Do you think Ellen and I are distanced, Dick?"

"I hope we didn't keep you up all night with our schtupping," Dick answers. He disengages a honeybun from the matched set in the bread basket. I smile into my o.j.

"Well, I slept beautifully, dear," Ma says. She starts to pour Dick's coffee with the spout in his cup. "I always do when my baby is in the house."

"Allow me." Dick takes the pot. He pours his own, lengthening and shortening the distance between pot and cup like a magician. Ma holds her breath. Her china is English and was designed in the eighteenth century for a blind nobleman. The pattern is raised so he could see it with his fingers.

I watch Dick watch Ma massage her cup.

"Your mother's a real sensualist," he says to me.

Ma opens her eyes. "Why thank you Dick dear," she says. "I take that as a compliment."

The house shakes. Dad lumbers down the stairs. Despite his size, he moves like a high school basketball player. He walks with a loose bounce, palms backward. He pivots on one heel when he turns. Ma whisks the bread basket into the kitchen.

"Morning," Dad says, munching the honeybun he has appropriated from my hand.

During the week Dad wears his judge's robes. During the weekend he wears black mail-order sweats. He seems to like loose black things. I stare at him and decide once and for all he is not fat. He is big. A big man. But not fat. Any thinner and he wouldn't look right. Dad's a type.

"I made you a nice grapefruit," Ma says.

"Only God can make a grapefruit." Dad winks at me.

"It took me a long time to find this grapefruit,

Harold. It's *organic*. This grapefruit has never been sprayed."

"Fern," Dick says. "Where on earth did you find an unsprayed grapefruit?"

Ma is studying Dad's hair, trying to decide if it's been combed.

"Well, that's my Fern," Dad says and digs in.

"How's your fern?" Dick asks.

"I never did understand that." Ma repositions tabletop items—salt, pepper, the Nutrasweet bowl.

"Best grapefruit I ever had," Dad says. "Better than my mother's grapefruit. Better than grapefruit before the war."

Ma shoots him a look.

"Do you have any honey?" he asks. "It's just a little sour."

"That's right, Harold. Anything to make it fattening."

"You want it broiled, Daddy?"

"Your father doesn't want broiled grapefruit. Your father wants to know why we don't hear from you."

"I don't?" Dad says. "We do?"

"Your father and I are tired of always being the ones to pick up the phone. We want to help if you're in trouble."

"I'm not in trouble," I say and wonder why she said that. Do I look like I'm in trouble? Am I in trouble and I don't know it? What does she know? I must be in trouble.

With no bread basket on the table, Dad heads for the Tiptree marmalade. He spreads some on his finger.

"Tell us, Ellen. What is it? We're your parents."

"Let me tell her," Dick says. "I'll tell her."

A thread of marmalade quivers on the underhang of Dad's lower lip. Ma sits down. Dick plays with his cup. "I've asked your daughter to marry me," he says.

"Why, that's wonderful. Just wonderful." Dad explodes out of his chair. He adds velocity by pressing his palms against the table. It's the only fat-man gesture in his repertoire. "That's wonderful news. Wonderful. Give Daddy a hug."

"And?" Ma says.

"And," Dick answers. "She gave me a firm maybe."

Dad looks puzzled.

"Harold," Ma says. "You're a judge and you don't know you're being set up?"

■

On the way back to the city, we follow Dad's car to the new Chinese restaurant. It's as narrow as a bowling lane with a single row of Formica-topped tables cramped against one wall. In the center of our table, what must be the last fly of the year whirrs in a circle on its back. The four of us stare at it. The fly is the loudest thing in the restaurant and it shows no sign of letting up. I flip it with my fingernail, but it goes back on its back. We stare at its blue belly until Ma takes the initiative and asks Dick what he'd like to have. He pretends to read the Chinese figures on the menu then says, "I'll have two lines with a squiggle, a tee with two crosses, and some upside-down Y with a line through the middle. No MSG."

Dad cracks up. Ma glares. "You think it's good for your father, laughing like that?"

We listen to the fly sizzle. Dick blows on it. The fly starts to paw the air as if it's running upside down. Then it rises straight up like a helicopter and lands on all sixes. It takes off as Dick and I soon do, heading back to the city and the apartment we have shared since the first pro-choice march.

.

"Marry me," Dick says staring at the road.

"And spoil it."

"Fruit spoils, not love."

I unbuckle my seat belt and slide over next to him. I turn my nose into his balding Shetland that smells like Royall Lyme, Armor All Car Wax, and something primitive. I inhale him, sucking him into my nose, down into my lungs, oxygenating my blood with him.

"She's so mean. I can't stand it."

"She adores him," Dick says.

"If I ever talk that way to you, shoot me. Inject an air bubble between my toes."

"He likes it. You don't see that? He doesn't need you to defend him."

I rest my hand on Dick's long corduroy leg. That tells him to stop talking. It starts to rain.

" 'I Heart Irish Setter Pups,' " Dick says. A Rabbit whizzes by. " 'I Heart Cambridge.' " Then a Toyota.

'I Left My Heart in Syracuse, New York.' 'I Brake for Whales.' 'Honk If You Heart Geese.' "

There has been no preparation for this rain. It submerges the car and covers us and I get for the moment the sensation that we are not moving. That we are fixed in water like two tiny figures in a snow globe.

"Do you trust me?" Dick says.

"More than anyone."

"Have I ever lied to you?"

"Not that I know of."

"Well will you believe me when I tell you you love me?"

We hear a siren. The police car's right behind us.

"Shit." Dick checks the speedometer. "Sixty-five. Fuck." He starts to pull over. A plain dark blue Chevy with a flashing red light on the dashboard swerves past us.

"Whew," I say, dropping my hand between Dick's legs. "Just when you think everything is fine, just when you think you're safe, something closes in on you."

"Ummmm." He puts his arm around me. "Unmarked love."

It's raining so hard we can't see anything. The headlights look like they're shining on a white sheet.

Dick makes a sharp turn. He takes us over a cliff and drives straight up until we're on top of the rain. I look down and see a slick black highway broken by headlights and taillights, streaks of red and white. Dick makes another turn and we're up among the stars.

"Love on Board," he says to me. "I Brake for Love."

The sky is dark and clear. Dick steers between the stars. He's a good driver. Wherever we're going he'll get us there.

Patricia Volk is the author of the novel *White Light*. Her previous collection of stories, *The Yellow Banana*, won the 1984 Word Beat Fiction Book Award. Her short fiction has appeared in the *Atlantic*, *Playboy*, the *Quarterly* and small presses. She is a frequent contributor to the *New York Times Magazine* and lives in New York with her husband and two children.

Printed in the United States
By Bookmasters